Weldon

born in England and raised in New Zealand. took degrees in Economics and Psychology at University of St Andrews in Scotland and after decade of odd jobs and hard times began writing fiction. She is well known as novelist, screenwriter cultural journalist. Her works include *The Life and Loves of a She-Devil*, *Big Women*, *Rhode Island Blues* and *The Bulgari Connection*, plus the acclaimed memoir of her early life, *Auto da Fay*.

Also by Fay Weldon

FAY WELDON

THE PRESIDENT'S CHILD

Flamingo
An Imprint of HarperCollins*Publishers*

Flamingo
An Imprint of HarperCollins*Publishers*
77–85 Fulham Palace Road,
Hammersmith, London W6 8JB

Flamingo® is a registered trademark of
HarperCollins*Publishers* Ltd

www.fireandwater.com

Published by Flamingo 2003

9 8 7 6 5 4 3 2 1

First published in Great Britain by
Hodder and Stoughton Ltd 1982
First published in paperback by Sceptre,
an imprint of Hodder and Stoughton Ltd 1993

Copyright © Fay Weldon 1982

Fay Weldon asserts the moral right to
be identified as the author of this work

This novel is entirely a work of fiction.
The names, characters and incidents portrayed in it are
the work of the author's imagination. Any resemblance to
actual persons, living or dead, events or localities is
entirely coincidental.

ISBN 0 00 710925 3

Set in Garamond 3 by
Rowland Phototypesetting Ltd,
Bury St Edmunds, Suffolk

Printed and bound in Great Britain by
Clays Ltd, St Ives plc

1

On Sunday afternoons, when the world pauses and waits for the next great event, when the streets are empty and unnaturally still and the weight of obligation hangs over the land, the residents of Wincaster Row come calling on me. They come out of kindness because I am blind; and out of kindness to them, in the desolation of Sunday afternoon, I gather past and present together and tell them stories.

Today I tell them about Isabel, who fell in love, and in so doing made the whole world falter and take a different turning.

Pit-pat, spitter-spat. Listen! How the rain blows against the window-pane. Easy to feel, on such a day and in such a place, that great events are nothing to do with us, that we are cut off from sources of worldly energy, that people and politics are entirely separate; that the mainstream of life is, in fact, a long way off.

'It isn't so,' I tell them. 'Isabel lived next door. The river flows at the end of the garden; what's more, it's deep, wide, muddy and tricky: not the tranquil flowing stream you might hope for. Isabel almost drowned!'

Pit-pat, spitter-spat. In the end we will all know more than we did before. Shouldn't that be enough to base a life upon?

The women of Wincaster Row don't agree, of course. The pursuit of knowledge clearly isn't enough for them. They want happiness, love, sex, good dinners, money, consumer durables, admiration, laughing children and goodness knows what else besides. They still live in the real world, and not in their heads.

We are all women today. Oliver the architect from No. 13 couldn't come, nor Ivor the alcoholic from No. 17. They had domestic commitments. So we have earth-mother Jennifer from No. 9, who is pregnant yet again; and cross Hilary, in serviceable jeans and clumpy boots, from No. 11; and pretty, clever little Hope from No. 25, fidgety for lack of sexual excitement, which she needs, or so Hilary complains, as a heroin addict needs a fix.

There are no even numbers in Wincaster Row. The demolition men got to that side of the street before the conservation society were able to step in – or rather lie down in the path of bulldozers. Hilary still limps, on a wet day, and now, listening to me, she rubs her damaged knee.

'Is it true about Isabel?' asks Hilary. 'Or will you be making it up?'

Hilary, Jennifer and Hope expect truth to be exact and finite. I know it is more like a mountain that has to be scaled. The peak of the mountain pierces the clouds and can only rarely be seen, and has never been reached. And

2

what you see of it, moreover, depends upon the flank of the mountain you stand upon, and how exhausted getting even so far has made you. Virtue lies in looking upwards, toiling upwards, and sometimes joyously leaping from one precarious crag of fact and feeling to the next.

'More or less true,' I say.

Isabel was my neighbour. She lived next door, and filled my world with life and energy and bustle. Now the house is empty, and weeds break through the pavings of the front path, where once little Jason, Isabel's son, played and grizzled and imposed his riotous will upon the world. The gate swings loose and creaks. Estate Agents have planted a 'For Sale' sign amongst the weeds: it stands like some kind of enemy tree, unexpectedly sprouted.

Pit-pat, spitter-spat. The river's nearer: it flows just outside the door. Keep the sandbags ready; who knows when the water will rise? Listen! It's raining harder than ever.

'It wouldn't surprise me if it was true,' says Jennifer. 'Isabel never quite fitted into Wincaster Row.'

'She was too perfect,' says Hope, 'if that's what you mean. She had it all made, unlike the rest of us. The perfect companionate marriage. The true, the new, the sharing!'

Though some of us think Hope has it all made: unmarried and self-supporting and no children, and not yet thirty, and prone to falling in love, and being fallen in love with: skipping up and down the Row, little and light, and remarking, from time to time, 'What I don't understand

3

is, since sex is so nice, why doesn't everyone do it *all the time?*'

Wincaster Row is in Camden Town, on the fringes of central London. It is an island of privilege in an underprivileged city sea. In the summer Bach and Vivaldi flow from open windows, over lawns and flowerbeds, keeping at bay the sound of police sirens and ambulance bells. In the winter, although the windows are closed, the sound of alarm comes nearer. A communal garden has been contrived out of dust and rubble. Oliver the architect, and Jennifer, who loves gardens, were instrumental in its creation, and so was Camden Council, which broods over these parts like some sort of touchy, monolithic god.

We are not perfect, here in Wincaster Row. We are not entirely rational or entirely noble or entirely forgiving. We have our fears and our angers and our points of obsession, like anyone else. But we are kind to our children, and each other; the struggle for self-improvement is assumed, and with the improvement of the self the improvement of the world. I think we are good people.

Pit-pat, spitter-spat. Don't mind the rain. The farmers need it. Pray it isn't radioactive.

We are not so much the salt of the world – salt is taken for granted these days – as the handful of mixed herbs which makes the meal at all possible. For the most part we are communicators – we teach, or work in television or films or publishing, or are in some way connected with theatre, or think we ought to be. We are social workers and diplomats and civil servants. We aspire to the truth.

4

We rattle round the mountain a fraction higher than the rest of the world. We are brave if we have to be: we will, if pushed, put public good before private profit. We would even die for a principle, unless it damaged the children.

We crawled up on to this island of civilisation, carried by tides we never quite understood; now we live better than we could ever have expected.

There are others like us all over the world – enclaves of aspiration in New Delhi and Sydney and Helsinki and Houston, and in all the big cities of the world; and little clusters of us in towns and villages everywhere – in Blandford, Dorset, and Moose Jaw, Saskatchewan, and Tashkent, Georgia, our goodwill crossing barriers of language and social organisation; a great upswell of the culture of kindness. We read each other's books, listen to each other's poems. On Sunday morning gatherings, at drinks-before-dinner time, in Moscow and Auckland and New York and Oslo and Manila, our children will be misbehaving, and anxious parental eyes will follow their noisy course about the room, wondering where error lies, and why it is that children reflect the parents' uncertainties, rather than their certainties. Self-doubt defines us, as well as aspiration.

At any gathering in Wincaster Row which included children, Isabel's Jason would be the noisiest and the roughest and the most disobedient. He was a blond, stocky child, with firm, well-covered limbs, a clear, high complexion and widely spaced, wandering blue eyes, which for a time needed glasses with one lens blacked out, to check the wandering. As a baby he had cried a good deal and slept very little. He was on his feet and breaking things by the

5

time he was a year old and speaking three months later, the better to say no. By the age of two he could tell his letters, but at six was still declining to read. He developed a tearful roar which he would use when thwarted, and a persistent self-pitying grizzle when he was bored or uncomfortable. He demanded, and he received, and was much loved.

Pit-pat, spitter-spat. Some children are more difficult to rear than others. Those most troublesome young grow up, eventually, to be the most co-operative and benign. That is the wisdom of Wincaster Row. If no one disciplines you, you do it yourself, eventually. Kropotkin said so, long ago.

Isabel and Homer said it to their neighbours, and each other. They shared the penances and triumphs of their beliefs, as they shared their lives, their income and the household chores. Isabel and Homer were partners in a New Marriage, in which all these things were shared, all things discussed. Up and down Wincaster Row we looked to Isabel and Homer to show us how to live, and worried because they didn't quite seem to belong. He came from America; she from Queensland, Australia.

Pit-pat, spitter-spat. Rain is an extra hazard to the blind. A stick will tell you where the kerb is, but very little about the depth of the puddle the other side. When it rains, I stay indoors. I have good friends, a solicitous husband, and one of those machines which, if spoken to, will type back a printed version of what was said for the sighted, and a Braille version for the personal use of the operator. Thank God for progress, the silicon chip, and money.

The rain blows harder against the window-pane. Hilary turns on my central heating; it's mid-summer but it's cold. Presages of what's to come! Surely men and women can be friends and lovers too? Be both parents and partners?

Homer and Isabel married because Jason was on the way. Isabel told me so, as she told me many private things. She was my good friend. When I first lost my sight it was Isabel who looked after me. My husband, Laurence, had often to be away. He is an investigative reporter: he fills up the back pages of newspapers, and is often away. Isabel guided me through the new, frightening dark, until I became accustomed to it. She was a good guide: she did not, at the time, understand fear; although later she was brought to it. She could not comprehend the terrors of my new place; she skated happily over practical surfaces, warning me of tangible objects – here a chair, there a step – and understandable events – you cannot read the telephone bill, but you can use the telephone to ask how much it is – ignoring the intangible, the horrific and the confusing – the voiceless shriekings and weepings and moanings in my head. There was a kind of obduracy in her that helped me; a startling common sense; a refusal, almost, to believe that going blind was a major event. She was blind to my blindness, in all but a practical sense.

And just as well, for so major an event did the failure of my sight appear, at first, to my husband, so filled were his own eyes with tears of guilt, remorse and pity, that for a time he could scarcely find his own way, let alone mine.

'For God's sake, Laurence,' Isabel would say, 'go back to the pub –' and he would stumble back, unshaven and morose, from whence he'd come, leaving Isabel to teach me how to comb my hair by touch and code my clothes, by feel, upon the shelves: and leaving me, of course, bereft of the comfort of Laurence's presence, however tiresome and maudlin he might be, however given he was to saying, 'Oh, it is useless, hopeless. It is not just the beginning of the end, it is the end itself. We had better just give up, and die together.'

Now that I can no longer see people I hold memories of their appearance in my mind. They appear on the pale sheet of my memory: black-edged, cut-out figures, clearly defined. Laurence stands looming in a doorway, outlined by the light, blocking it out: sensuous, thick-set and fleshy: facing me, four-square: then he turns his head so that the light catches his face and his eyes are as wide and his cheeks as delicate as a girl's.

Isabel lies upon a stone slab, hands folded in prayer, like some carved saint who achieved great glory in life and is remembered in death. Light from stained glass windows shines upon her imperfect profile, and glances off her long, broad-hipped body, the breasts unduly flattened after Jason's birth. Then in my vision she sits up, and turns and smiles at me, and rises and stretches, confident and proud of her body, and saunters off, in so modern and careless a fashion as to put all thoughts of graven knights and saintliness out of my mind.

When she is gone the church is cold and empty and I am left in the dark again.

Isabel's profile is imperfect because when she was nine she was kicked in the jaw by a horse her mother loved.

'Don't fuss,' said her mother.

The Flying Doctor did, however. Isabel and her mother lived far into the Australian outback and were dependent upon rather makeshift medical arrangements. The doctor flew in, and wired and stitched and re-firmed teeth, and all would have been well had the horse not got her in the jaw a second time, barely a week later.

'For Christ's sake,' said her mother, 'what do you do to that horse?'

Here and now, sisters. Here and now. Build your houses strong and safe, love your children, and die for them if you have to, and try to love your mothers, who didn't.

'I patted its rump,' said Isabel. 'The way you told me I should.' But her mother wasn't listening. She was on the phone, getting a message through to the Flying Doctor.

'I feel a right Charlie,' she said.

The wet season was upon Harriet and Isabel by then: the helicopter carrying the Flying Doctor back crash-landed, and the doctor was injured. The yellow mud rose up around: if you went out in the rain your head hurt. The new injuries to Isabel's jaw got forgotten, one way and another: her chin thereafter protruded too much and her mouth was flattened, and her teeth leaned backward, and joggled together; the doctor lost an eye and a leg. Isabel felt the responsibility of it all, but thereafter, having survived that, dreaded none. And the imperfection of the bottom half of her face, compared to the cool, gracious, wide-eyed perfection of the rest of it, gave her a quirky charm when she was young and a

9

look of intelligence as she grew older. She inspired love as much as lust, in the souls of the young outback boys, who roamed in packs across the desert in that for the most part loveless land.

Pit-pat, spitter-spat. Rain in London is safe and mild, for anyone, that is, except the blind. It beats upon hard pavements and rolls away down drains. It doesn't drown the world in yellow mud.

'It's no life for you here,' said Isabel's mother when her daughter was fifteen. 'Not someone like you. You'd better get out.'
'Come with me,' said Isabel. They were all each other had.
'There's the horses,' said Isabel's mother. 'I can't leave them.'

Of course. Isabel had forgotten, momentarily, about her mother having the horses. They weren't splendid horses; they were rather shaggy, moulting, ailing animals, plagued by a hundred insect pests, who did nothing but stand reproachfully in a field and consume what was left of Isabel's patrimony, in sacks of feed and vet's bills. They kicked up dust in the summer, and stirred up mud in the winter.

Isabel's mother loved them; and Isabel tried to love them for her mother's sake, and failed. Chatto and Windus and Heinemann and Warburg and Herbert and Jenkins – (Secker died, of a snake bite). Memories, all, of Isabel's mother's past. Isabel's mother grew up in literary London and was swept out of it and into the outback by Isabel's father, who farmed and was Australian. Presently he went off to war and never came back, preferring life in a grass hut with a Malaysian girl to life with Isabel's mother and Isabel. Mother and child stayed where they were, selling off land, thousand acre by thousand acre, until there was nothing left but the wormy wooden house with its rickety balcony, and the six horses in a single field, and the snakes sleeping in the tindery undergrowth, and Isabel's mother, dusty and yellowy, grown into the landscape.

Where else was she to go, what else was she to do? Pinned down by war, world events, her own stubborn nature, and a baby? When it rained it was as if she called down the heavens to avenge her, and if they drowned her doing it, so be it. *Pit-pat, spitter-spat.*

'But what will you do?' Isabel asked her mother, 'when I'm gone?'
'What I've always done,' said her mother. 'Look at the horizon.'

Isabel thought her mother would be glad when she had gone: that her mother had done her duty by her. That though she, Isabel, felt great intimacy with her mother, her mother did not feel the same for her. The child is accidental to the mother. The mother is integral to the child. It is a painful lesson for the child to learn.

Secker's body had gone to the knackers; all except the head, which Isabel's mother had had stuffed and put in the hall. It rolled glass eyes at Isabel the day she left home, while the flies buzzed about it. Secker was the horse responsible for Isabel's lopsided jaw: her mother had wept when he died, swollen horribly.

11

'Why are you crying?' asked Isabel, at the time. She had never known her mother cry before.

'Everything went wrong,' said her mother. 'It was the war. And how could I go back afterwards? Everyone would have said "I told you so". They never wanted me to marry your father. They all said it wouldn't work.'
'What everyone?'
'Everyone,' said her mother, desolately.

And who indeed was everyone? Harriet's friends and family had scattered. That was what war did. It took families by the scruff of their neck and shook them and tossed them in the air, and didn't even bother to see where they fell, as the farm dogs did with rats.

But Isabel's mother hadn't been there to see the war, of course. War rolled across far continents, killing everything it touched. Isabel's mother just sat and gazed at an unchanging, yellow horizon, over which a red sun rose and fell, and the people of her past had atrophied in her mind, set in their condemning ways. Would anyone bother now to say, 'I told you so'? Of course not. Or was there anyone left to say it? Isabel's mother could hardly know any more. She never answered letters, and presently they'd stopped coming.

Now she wept over Secker, who had ruined her daughter's face; but saved her character.

'It's unlucky to be beautiful,' Harriet said to Isabel, once. 'If you are, some man just comes along and marries you and stops you making your way in the world.'

The hot sun and the hard rain had turned Harriet's skin to leather, and stubbornness had set her mouth askew, and her eyes were red-rimmed from staring at the horizon. But once she had been beautiful. Isabel thought she was still beautiful. And so, no doubt, thought Isabel's father, long ago.

Isabel's mother wouldn't talk about Isabel's father. 'He did what he wanted,' was the most she ever said, 'the way all men do.'

Isabel thought he must have been strong, to have farmed so many acres on his own, and powerful, to rule over it. She thought he must have been one of the natural lords of that land: tall, lean, bronzed, mean, with features sharpened by the hot wind: packs of dogs and horses and lesser men scurrying at their heels. The lesser men were red from Foster's and rendered stupid, if they hadn't been to begin with, by the coarseness and ignorance in which they traded. If there was a flower, they trod it underfoot, and laughed. If there was a dog, they kicked it. That was why the dogs snarled and snapped.

She could not see her mother with that kind of man. Her mother saw visions, too, Isabel was sure of it. Her mother saw something of the infinite in the yellow dust, or in the rusty clouds swirling over the flat land, that sometimes illuminated her face and made her sigh with pleasure.

'What's the matter?' asked Isabel the little girl. 'Is there something out there?'
'Something more than I can tell,' said Isabel's mother,

averting her eyes from the horizon, scraping away at burnt, thin-bottomed saucepans.

Isabel tore a leg off her favourite doll, smeared it with mutton fat, and gave it to the dogs to chew.

Isabel told me so. She never confessed it to anyone else; not Homer her husband, and certainly not Jason her son. I am blind and can be trusted not to condemn.

Pit-pat, spitter-spat. Jennifer has made tea. Hilary offers me a plate of biscuits.

'Chocolate chip a.m.: lemon sandwiches p.m.,' she says, describing the plate to me.

I take the chocolate chip from nine o'clock. Lemon sandwiches flake all over the carpets, and though the blind can vacuum clean it is not a very efficient process. Hope brought them with her. She should have known better.

I have been blind for two years. I crossed a road without looking. A car hit me behind the knees. I bounced on to its bonnet and off again, cracking my head on the kerb, somewhere to the left of the medulla; in the area which controls the sight. The blow did unspecified damage which means my eyes simply fail to register what they see. The fact intrigues surgeons and eye specialists and indeed psychiatrists, and I am forever up at the hospital while they peer and probe and inject and intrude. They did an operation which left the left side of my right hand insensitive to hot and cold, but achieved nothing except my pain and terror and humiliation. Occasionally some irritable physician will remark, 'I am sure you could see if you wanted to.'

There are ranks in blindness, of course, like anything else. I, being slightly mysterious in my plight, almost wilful, and my eyes looking pretty much like anyone else's, come high up on the scale. A noble blindness. To have been born blind, or to have gone blind through illness, ranks lower. A pitiful, punitive blindness. The sense that God afflicts us at our birth because we deserve it is strong. The millions of India live by the notion, after all.

An accident, however! Accidents happen to everyone. They are dramatic and exciting; children love them, and the wearing of the plaster that signifies calamity. I ran into the street because I had had a quarrel with my husband Laurence, and I didn't see the car coming because I was crying, or perhaps because I didn't want to.

Listen to the rain against the window! Summer rain. Each drop is a lost human soul, driven by winds it cannot comprehend, trying to get in here where it is safe and warm, where we gather our infirmities together and make the most of what we have. Be grateful for the glass that saves you from the force of such savagery and discontent. Drape it with curtains; polish it on fine days; try not to see too much, but just enough for survival's sake. Preserve your peace of mind. There is not much time; all things end in death. Do not lament the past too much, or fear the future too acutely, or waste too much energy on other people's woes, in case the present dissolves altogether.

These things Isabel taught me in spite of herself. Little by little, she revealed herself and her story to me. *Pit-pat, spitter-spat*. Draw the curtain.

2

On Jason's sixth birthday Isabel woke with the feeling that something was wrong. She was launched suddenly into consciousness, one second lying in dreams, the next starting into alertness. She thought perhaps there was an intruder in the room, but of course there was not. Homer lay beside her as usual on the brass bed, on his side, relaxed and peaceful, legitimate and uxorious, the delicate skin of his eyelids stretched fine over his mildly prominent eyes. His face had the vulnerable, slightly raw look that faces do, which go bespectacled by day and naked by night.

He slept quietly. He always did. A man with a clear conscience, thought Isabel. Not weltering and hiding deep down somewhere beneath the levels of consciousness — but neatly and tidily, just below the surface, afraid of nothing because he had done no wrong. If Homer slept, what could be amiss?

Something. Jason? No. If she listened hard, as now she did, she could hear the rhythmic change in the stillness which meant that Jason too slept soundly in the room above.

Nothing unusual was happening outside in Wincaster Row. It was half-past six, too early for the milkman, the paper-boy or the postman: those ritual early callers who come like the sun, to remind each household that it is not alone but owes a living, perforce, to the rest, and must soon get up and make it. Well, time enough.

The fright that woke Isabel did not diminish with the discovery that there was no cause for it; rather it intensified into a profounder apprehension: the feeling that something terrible was about to happen.

Work? But what could happen there? She had so far presented four late-night programmes for the BBC: they had gone successfully; she had a new two-year contract; the work was comparatively easy. True, it involved the professionalisation of the self, every Monday night, the handing over of the persona for consumption by millions; but that came easily enough, and was forgotten by Tuesday afternoon. Even if her contract was cancelled, and she was ignominiously dismissed, she would not see that as disastrous but as a practical problem. This sudden new fear, now so powerful that it made her catch her breath and hug her chest, had nothing to do with practicalities.

Jason's birthday? In the afternoon he was to have an outing to the cinema with five school friends. That, although nothing to look forward to, was surely nothing to fear. In fact Homer was to return early from the office and take them to the cinema, while she would stay home and ice the cake and cut little sandwiches into animal shapes. The division of labour was fair, and had been accomplished, as usual, without acrimony.

'It's true I'll get to see the film,' said Homer, 'and you won't. But watching *Superman II* with five six-year-olds is a dubious pleasure. You're sure you don't want to do it the other way round?'

'No,' said Isabel. 'Besides, you'd make the sandwiches with brown bread in spite of it being Jason's birthday.'

'Jason's digestion doesn't know it's his birthday,' said Homer.

Nothing there, surely, to have her sitting up in alarm in her lacy white bed, in the safety of the dark, green-papered walls, the gilt mirrors on the walls throwing back images only of what was familiar and loved.

Isabel got out of bed and went upstairs to Jason's bedroom. She, who once slept in the nude, now slept in a nightie – as do the mothers of wakeful children – which served as dressing gown as well.

Jason slept on his back, arms outflung, an expression of benign calm on his face. At the foot of his bed were stacked presents, wrapped by Homer and herself the night before.

Jason's American grandparents had sent a cowboy suit in real leather, with silver-plated holsters and guns.

'Should we?' said Homer. 'Guns?'

'It's his birthday,' said Isabel. 'And everyone else does. And research shows that children deprived of the formalised expression of aggression via fantasy perform more aggressive acts than children not so deprived.'

'How convenient,' said Homer. But the guns were beautifully made, light, delicately filigreed, and Jason would be

19

proud of them. So Homer sighed and added them to the pile.

There was no present from Harriet in Australia. There never was.

'I don't think my mother is a woman at all,' Isabel had said to Homer the night before. 'Not now. Once she was, but now she's turned herself into the trunk of an old gum tree, and the sand has silted her up.' Homer had kissed Isabel and held her hand and said nothing, for there was nothing to be said.

Harriet! Of course, that was it. Something wrong! Isabel went downstairs to the living room – the two ground floor rooms made into one – where the blinds were still down, and the two companionable glasses still stood from the night before, and three half-smoked cigarettes, evidence of Homer's attempts to give up smoking by the idiosyncratic and expensive method of smoking less and less of each cigarette he lit. She telephoned Australia. She could dial direct now: she did not need the intermediary of a telephonist. Twelve numbers, and there was her mother, and her past.

The telephone rang and rang in her mother's house, unanswered. The instrument stood in the window sill by the front porch, and whenever it rang grains of sand would jump and bounce around its base in a dance of amazement. Isabel had watched them, many times. Perhaps my mother is lying there on the kitchen floor, she thought, on the other side of the fly screen, and that's why she doesn't answer. She's dead, or had a stroke, or a heart attack; or she's been raped and robbed; or perhaps she has a boyfriend at last and stays out nights.

A tune rang through her head. A folk singer had sung it on last week's show:

> *'Bad news is come to town,*
> *Bad news is carried,*
> *Some say my love is dead,*
> *Some say he's married.'*

Or perhaps she no longer answers the phone. Eight years since I last saw her. She has sunk finally back into herself; allows me to live her life for her.

The ringing stopped. Her mother said hello.

'Hello, Mother.'
'Oh, it's you, Isabel. How are you, chicken?'
'I'm fine.'
'Everything OK? Husband, kid and so on?'
'Yes, they're fine.'
Silence. Then:
'It's very late at night. I was in bed.'
'I'm sorry, Mum. I just wanted to make sure you were all right.'
'Why shouldn't I be? Nothing ever changes here. How about your end?'
'I have my own TV show. Once a week. It's only a chat show, but it's a start.'
'Good on you, chicken. Given up journalism, have you? Or did it give you up?'
'It's the same thing, really.'

'Is it? I don't watch much TV; I wouldn't know. It all seems rather crude to me. But this is Australia, isn't it. Down under, here. Enjoy it, do you?'

'Yes.'

'That's the main thing. Homer doesn't mind?'

'No. Why should he?'

'You know what men are. What suits you never suits them. Listen, chicken, I hate to do this to you, but there's some sort of goddamned hornet got through the hole in the fly door. This place is rusting to pieces. I've got to go.'

'Of course, Mother. Is it big?'

'Very.'

'It's Jason's birthday today.'

'Jason? Oh, the little boy. He must be – what? Four, five? Give him my love. I'm not much use as a granny, but at least I exist.'

'At least you exist. Bye, Mum.'

'Why don't you just call me Harriet? Bye, sweetheart.'

Isabel crept back into bed, dry-mouthed, tasting dust and ashes. Everything was possible, yet everything was impossible. She could wring what she wanted out of the world – success and wealth and personal happiness – and it would do her no good. Her mother would always stand somewhere at the periphery of her vision, out of touch but never quite out of sight, watching her efforts and smiling, passing on the knowledge that the old would do better to keep to themselves – that in the end all goods must be pointless and all sweets tasteless. Better be deaf, and lame, and blind, than know these things too young.

Homer turned towards her in the bed. 'What's the matter?'

'I don't know.'

'What's the time?'

'Early.'

'Where have you been?'

'Ringing my mother.'

'Christ, why?'

'It's Jason's birthday.'

'What did she say?'

'Not what I wanted her to say.'

'What was that?'

'Well done. Congratulations. I miss you. Why don't you fly out and see me. The things your mother says to you.'

Homer enclosed her body, as he did her mind, the better to drive out doubt. He folded her in lean, well-exercised arms. He weighed, year in, year out, exactly what the chart at the doctor's surgery said he should, increasing or decreasing his calorie intake as the need arose. He cycled to his office every weekday morning, and cycled home again every evening. Twice a week, on Tuesdays and Thursdays, he rose early and ran almost the entire circuit of Regent's Park.

'I would live for ever if I could,' he would say. 'As I can't, I will live as long as I can.'

He is a happy man, thought Isabel, he must be. And she wondered what it would be like, to have such an appetite for sheer existence, and when they made love, would try to catch it from him: but the very evenness of his temperament somehow prevented there being a surplus of whatever it was he had; he kept it to himself: worked upon her physically and rhythmically, and left it to her to create the heights and depths she felt appropriate, which, indeed,

23

she did create and felt no disappointment in him, and could answer, in truth, were anyone impertinent enough to ask for details of her love life, 'Why yes, it is very good. At any rate, neither of us looks elsewhere for partners.'

Homer's body was as neat and orderly as his mind. It smelt sweet. Her response to it was easy and immediate. She trusted him. Homer did one thing at a time. She liked that. When he made love he focused his energies and concentrated upon the action of body against the body within, as if the least he could do for his partner was to keep the messiness of emotion out, to offer himself clean and whole and untired and uncluttered. The show of emotion, affection, came before and after. It was Isabel's nature to do everything all at once: to concentrate the emotions of the day in herself, however inchoate and troublesome and tumultuous, and open her legs at night and be taken body and soul. And because she offered both, he took both, body and soul: but to her he offered one at a time. Body first – this, and this, like this, firm and decisive – soul after, icing on a cake, made a little too thin, slipping and sliding and insecure. 'Was that all right, Isabel?' And she would say yes, yes, of course, never quite recovering from one night to the next that he found it necessary to ask. What was, was.

He never cried out aloud in orgasm: the noise was stifled, as if there were always listeners, watchers. 'Hush, hush,' he'd say to her, if they were away and the bed creaked: or even at home, when she forgot, when something – perhaps only the accumulated emotions of the day – required a wilder protest, noisier relief. And since they were not the emotions he, Homer, had engendered, she had no real right to them at such a time, and so was readily hushed.

Sometimes, after they'd made love, she would weep and not know why.
'What's the matter?' he'd ask.
'I don't know.'
'Didn't I do it right?' he would ask, slipping and sliding into insecurity, and she would laugh, because he so patently did do it right, and brought her such gratification.
'Of course you do it right,' she'd say.
'Then what is it?'

But she couldn't say. Perhaps she wept for the sorrows of the world, or because all things end in death, or because she could not experience pleasure without experiencing too the pain of knowing it must end, or perhaps she wept because Homer never did.

Today at least there was an easy answer.
'I'm crying because my mother upset me,' she said. 'I wish she loved me more.'
'I wish my mother loved me less,' said Homer. 'Then I wouldn't feel so responsible for her.'
'We've both run out on them.'
'Run out?' said Homer in surprise. 'I like to feel I've run in.'

Sometimes disagreeable people would suggest to Homer that he had run out on his country; that his anti-Vietnam stand made him anti-American: that living in Europe was a form of treachery to the country that had nurtured him.

'If you say so,' Homer would say, easily. 'I guess you're right. I'd rather the world was my oyster, than America, in its present mood, was my country. I'm doing nothing illegal. I pay my taxes. I just like it over here.'

But now that self-doubt and national guilt suffused the American soul as much as they did the European, he crossed the Atlantic more easily. He went to the States some three or four times a year, about his employer's business, or to take Jason to visit his grandparents.

'I know they support the handgun lobby,' he'd say, 'and so on and so forth, but a breath of air-conditioning and general efficiency can be quite stimulating.'

Isabel, unsure of her welcome, never went home to Australia. Sometimes she wondered, had Jason been a girl, whether Harriet would not have taken more interest in her grandchild.

'Don't worry,' Homer would say. 'We've made London our home, so let it be. We'll build our dynasty downwards; we'll forget what has gone before. Our past lies in our genes – that should be more than enough.'

Jason, the child of the continents, played happily in Wincaster Row, and wanted no other life.

Jason's birthday – upstairs, Jason woke and yelled his greeting to the world. It was not his custom to meet the day with quiet murmurs or gentle moans, as did to all accounts the children of Homer and Isabel's friends; rather, he liked to hail it with a shout of mixed elation and reproach.

Having released, as it were, the pent-up noise and passion of the night, he would then fall back into sleep for some five minutes before waking, permanently, for the second time. This time his yell would demand acknowledgement: it would go on until one or other of his parents appeared in his room.

'I expect he'll calm down when he reaches sexual maturity,' Homer would say, 'and has something else to do with the night and his energy.'

'Five minutes' grace,' he said this morning, dabbing away at Isabel's tears.

It was Homer's turn to see to Jason, but since it was his birthday both parents went. Isabel got out of her side of the bed; Homer got out of his. They pulled on jeans, and T-shirts, and sneakers. The telephone rang. It was one of Isabel's researchers, apologising for the earliness of the call, asking permission to contact a Norwegian architect breaking a world tour in London that day. Isabel's anxiety disappeared. The world was back to normal. There were decisions to be made, money to be earned, the world to be mastered.

Homer opened Jason's door: 'Pa-ra-pa-ra-pa-ra,' rattled Jason, firing his new filigreed gun at his parents, machine-gun style. 'I'm six, I'm nearly seven, I don't have to go to school today.'

'Yes, you do,' they said. Jason yelled and screamed and stamped. His parents reasoned and explained and cajoled.

Homer took Jason to school on Mondays and Wednesdays and collected him on Tuesdays and Thursdays. Isabel took him on Tuesdays and Thursdays and collected him on Mondays and Wednesdays. On Fridays both parents took him and collected him. The routine suited everyone.

Jason rode behind Homer on the bicycle when the weather was fine. Today was a bicycle day. Jason, still tear-stained, turned round to smile at his mother as they rode off. It was the smile of a prince to a courtier, immensely kind and immensely gracious. It was all-forgiving. It was clear to Isabel that he had always meant to go to school.

Isabel returned to the kitchen for coffee. The radio was on. The news had begun. Isabel listened half-professionally, half as an innocent citizen. She knew a sufficient number of journalists, had met enough editors, had worked on the fringes of enough news rooms, to know the processes by which balance was evolved: the half-accidental, half-purposeful ways in which bias was created, and truth, once again, slipped through the fingers and scattered, like a drop of mercury splashing on the floor: elusive in the first place, now gone for ever. Today some things were clear enough.

The long haul up to the American Presidential election had begun. The Primaries were under way. An outsider, the young Senator from Maryland, was looking good for the Democrats. His name was Dandridge Ivel – commonly known as Dandy Ivel. The commentator, speaking over a crackly line, was speculating on the advantages of having youth at the American helm again, harking back to the Kennedy era, and Camelot, and the golden age of the USA, before national shame, depression, monetarist policies, inflation, unemployment and street riots became common-place topics of conversation. The age before responsibility – the adolescence of a nation. Perhaps the USA could be young and vigorous again, with Dandy Ivel at the helm? The commentator, his enthusiasm bouncing and crackling off some ill-functioning satellite, left no doubt that he was a Dandy Ivel fan.

Isabel sat down. The house was quiet. The big school clock on the kitchen wall ticked with one rhythm: the grand-father clock in the hall, proud amongst the bicycles and coats, ticked with another. The school clock had to be wound, every day; the grandfather clock every eight. It was Isabel's job to wind the former, because she so easily forgot the latter. Homer never forgot.

She made herself a cup of coffee. Homer limited himself to two cups a day, and never drank the powdered kind. He feared the powdering agent was carcinogenic.

How would she ever live without Homer, who structured her life and surrounded her personality, and had made her lie-about, sleep-around personality into something so sure, so certain? Isabel clutched her arms across her chest. She had a pain. She rocked to and fro.

Of course she had known: she had seen or heard some mention somewhere of Dandy Ivel's name, and repressed the knowledge. Of course she had woken up afraid; of course she had rung her mother; of course she had wept.

Dandy Ivel, President of the United States.

29

Once, Isabel thought, I believed that events were haphazard and unrelated. I believed that people could be loved and left, and that happenings receded into the past and were gone, and that only with marriage, or its equivalent, and the birth of children, did the real, memorable, responsible life begin. Now she saw it was not so. Nothing was lost, not even the things you most wanted to lose. All things move towards a certain point in time. Our future is conditioned by our past: all of it, not just the paths we choose, or are proud of.

There was nothing to be done except say nothing, do nothing, hug the knowledge to herself. All would yet be well.

After an earthquake a house changes. Ornaments stand minutely different on the shelves; books lean at delicately altered angles. The lamp hangs quiet again at the end of its cord, but all things have discovered motion: the power to act and upset. The house laughs. You thought I was yours, your friend. You thought you knew me, but see, you don't. One day I may fall and crush you to death. It seemed to Isabel that the house she loved so much had changed. It mocked her, and laughed.

Isabel went next door to drink her coffee with Maia. Maia had quarrelled with her husband and run out into the street with tears in her eyes and stepped in front of a car, and lost her sight. Nothing is safe. Husbands, tears, cars, eyes. They won't be sorry; you will.

Maia and Isabel talked, and said nothing very important. During the day Isabel went into her Hello-Goodnight office. Alice, the researcher, had found the Norwegian

30

architect, but it transpired that these days he built underground houses, not solar-powered holiday homes. In consultation with the producer, Andrew Elphick, it was agreed that it would do neither the architect nor the programme any good were he to appear on it.

'We're an informative but light-hearted show,' said Elphick. 'Our viewers don't want to switch off Hello-Goodnight and have nuclear nightmares about the end of the world. They're common enough without us helping. Don't you agree, Isabel? I don't mind us being serious about feminism, racism, homosexuality or any of the other social trimmings, but I won't devalue the currency of the end of the world in a late-night chat show.'

Isabel saw what he meant. So did Alice, who was thirty-two, and had just turned her back on promotion in order to work just one more time, every time, with Elphick, whom she loved. Elphick was tall and broad and sad and clever and had red hair and a boyish smile. He was forty, and married. He was not popular with the camera crews or studio staff, at whom he shouted and raged, as if married to them.

'Isabel,' he said to her as she left the room, 'do you have a social conscience?'
'Of course,' she replied, startled.
'I thought you did,' he replied. 'It's rather like mine. We know where our duty lies. It's to fiddle as prettily as possible while Rome burns, so that Nero throws us a penny or two.'

He was drinking already. It was his occupation on five days out of seven. On the other two, run-up days and recording days, he kept sober. His face was lined by scars – from going, rumour said, through too many car windscreens. He only ever slept with Alice when he was drunk – and was thus able to keep his sober self, his real self, faithful to his wife. He believed in individual probity and sexual responsibility, and would not have shifty or immoral people on his show.

'The example of achievement,' he would say. 'That's what the people need to see. The power of the individual to shape his own destiny.'

'Her,' said Isabel, in duty bound.
'Or her,' he said, bored.

He caught Isabel's hand and kissed it, as she left, pressing it to his cold lips. She felt he was desperate rather than lecherous, and removed her hand gently.
'You don't really like me, do you?' he said. 'No one I like likes me. They put up with me but they don't like me.'

'Alice likes you,' said Isabel.

Isabel went home in time to receive Jason and his friends. The television was on. The video played an endless stream of Popeye cartoons. Parents came and failed to go. Isabel, after all, was a celebrity. Homer, unusually, was late home. The noise was great: Jason paced up and down in the way he had when impatient or cross, head bent forward, hands clasped behind his back, like some adult in a ridiculous cartoon. It made the grown-ups laugh, and that made Jason crosser.

'Daddy's late,' he said. 'We'll miss the film. It's no laughing matter.'

Which made them laugh the more, to hear the adult phraseology from the child's lips.

Jason's friend Bobby, who could never be trusted near anything technological, flicked the switch on the video which sent it back to transmitted television. There, on the screen, pacing up and down, head bent forward, hands clasped behind his back, against a background of the stars and stripes, was Dandy Ivel.

'For all the world like Jason,' remarked Bobby's mother. 'Isn't that a coincidence!'
'Stop walking about like that, Jason,' said Isabel.
'Why?' asked her son, not stopping.
'It's sloppy,' said Isabel.
'I think it's rather cute,' said Bobby's mother.
Jason's mother slapped her son on the cheek just as Homer came in.

'Isabel!' cried Homer, shocked.
'I'm sorry,' said Isabel, to both Jason and Homer. It was hard to say which one of them looked more hurt.

Homer switched off the television and ushered the children into a waiting taxi. Isabel iced the cake, while Bobby's mother watched, critically. Isabel wished Bobby's mother would go home, but she didn't. She stayed to help and cut the bread for the elephant sandwiches; she cut far too thickly and failed to butter the slices to the edges.

'Do you suffer much from premenstrual tension?' asked Bobby's mother.

She wore a lacy peasant blouse and a full cotton flowered skirt.

'No,' said Isabel, shortly.

'I never saw you hit Jason before. And he wasn't doing anything wrong, was he? I just thought it might be PMT. If men had to suffer from it they'd soon do something about it. I sometimes hit Bobby when I'm suffering. I'm sure most women do.'

'Happy Birthday Jason,' wrote Isabel, in green icing, by means of a rolled paper spill fastened with a safety pin.

'A pity Jason isn't older. He could enter a Dandy Ivel double competition.'

'I hardly think so,' said Isabel. 'He's fair and Dandy Ivel looks fairly dark to me.'

'Jason has the kind of hair that'll get darker as he grows older,' said Bobby's mother, getting the elephant shape wrong. 'I'm afraid these sandwiches look more like hedgehogs than elephants.'

'Anyway,' said Isabel, 'I think Ivel will fade into insignificance pretty quickly. I hardly think he'll get the presidential nomination.'

'I think he will,' said Bobby's mother. 'I did an evening

course in political sociology. I think the women of America are longing for a husband figure. They haven't had one since Kennedy. Dandy Ivel looks like the kind of man who'd take care of you.'

Homer came home with six frazzled children. They loved the sandwiches and ignored the cake. Jason threw jelly at the wall. He was over-excited. The parents came early and stood around drinking sherry. The children quarrelled over going-home presents. Bobby set up a roar, in the cloakroom. 'I'm afraid Jason must have bitten him,' Homer came back to apologise. Bobby's mother took him huffily home, saying she always slapped for biting. Bobby had been a biter, but not for long. She'd seen to that. Scratching was one thing, biting another.

'It's not good,' said Homer, when all had departed, supper had been eaten and night fallen. 'Jason *is* aggressive.'

'Perhaps it's the lead in the London water,' said Isabel.

'No,' said Homer. 'No excuses. I think he's disturbed.'

'Disturbed!' cried Isabel. 'That's ridiculous!'

'Isabel,' said Homer, 'face it. He watched *Superman II* from the aisle, and when the usherette tried to make him sit in a seat he bit her ankle. There was a terrible scene.'

Isabel laughed.

'It isn't a laughing matter,' said Homer. 'I think he should see a child psychologist.'

35

'What – Jason?'

'It can't do any harm, Isabel.'

'I suppose not,' said Isabel, but already she was terrified.

She had seen Jason as an extension of herself: flesh of her flesh, mind of her mind. But of course he was not. Jason, her child, was separated from her; the umbilical cord had been cut long ago but she had scarcely noticed. He no longer slept, ate, smiled, felt at her command. He did these things at his own prompting, not hers. She could no longer tuck him under her arm and run, should the going get bad. He could blame her for her decisions, dislike her for what she did, withdraw his love from her. Week by week he became less her perfect child and more his own imperfect master; yet still must suffer, as all children must suffer, because his mother's love for him was not perfect either: had fallen away, in the light of his own growing independent will, from its moment of perfection, somewhere at the beginning.

Now here was Homer, who should love Jason, saying their son was imperfect and disturbed, implying the fault was hers. She could not protect Jason, because he was not hers to protect, being six and his own self. And she could not protect herself, because she was guilty.

'Isabel,' said Homer, alarmed by the expression on her face, 'it's no big deal. I just thought it might help. It does seem to me that Jason isn't all that happy. We might be doing something wrong, between us. God knows what it is.

Perhaps it's seeing you on the television screen when you ought to be here in the house.'

'Ought to be?'

'From Jason's point of view, no one else's. Christ, Isabel, he's a kid of five.'

'Six.'

'Six. And Isabel, you're under a strain yourself.'

'Me?'

'You slapped the poor child. Slapped him! And why? What was he doing wrong?'

'Homer, I told him not to do something and he just went on doing it. There was a room full of screaming kids and bleating adults. I didn't slap him hard, just enough so he'd listen.'

'What was he doing?'

'I can't even remember. It wasn't important. Homer, Jason and I are well within the limits of ordinary normal mother and child behaviour. Most mothers slap their children from time to time.'

'I don't think that's true.'

'Most children are rude, aggressive, disobedient and defiant some of the time.'

'I don't think that's true either. And most children don't refuse to sit in their cinema seat and then bite the usherette's ankle when she tries to move them. There, you're smiling! I think you're acting something out through Jason, Isabel, really I do, and Jason is reacting badly to it.'

'You mean I should see an analyst?'

'Heaven forbid,' said Homer, wearily, and Isabel felt she had been unreasonable.

'Anyway,' said Isabel, 'we don't know any child shrinks. They're out of fashion.'

'I can always find out through my office,' said Homer. 'What's ten years out of date for you TV people, we publishers are just about cottoning on to.'

'Homer,' said Isabel, 'I get the feeling you resent my job. Shouldn't we be talking about that, and not shifting the whole problem on to poor little Jason?'

'I think,' said Homer, 'we are nearer to having a row than we ever have been. Let's go to bed.'

Homer and Isabel went to their white lacy bed with its delicate brass tracery at head and foot, in a bedroom with dark green walls and purple blinds. It was tidy because Homer kept it so. Isabel tended to leave her clothes where they fell. But she made the bed every day, lovingly and neatly, and even sometimes ironed the cotton sheets, when they came from the washing machine, because they were so pretty.

Homer forgave Isabel more quickly than Isabel forgave Homer. Or so it seemed. In fact, it was fear that kept Isabel lying stiffly on her back, her flesh shrinking from her husband's, and not anger at all. But he was not to know that. 'What's the matter?' said Homer. 'Look, if it so upsets you I'll never mention the matter of Jason and a shrink again.'

'Good,' said Isabel.

'Then turn round and kiss me.'

'No. I can't. I don't know why.'

'You see,' said Homer, 'it wasn't only that he bit the usherette and there was this fuss, but afterwards he denied it. He really honestly didn't seem to remember it. That was what really got me. I don't think the other kids noticed much. It was the bit when Superman throws the villain into the Coca-Cola sign. It was actually a shockingly violent film – not at all like *Superman I*, which was innocent.'

'Sometimes,' said Isabel, 'I get the feeling we're all being softened up for something, children and all.'

'If we are,' said Homer, 'there's nothing we can do about it, except look after our own.'

Isabel went to sleep and dreamed about the end of the world. Missiles flashed to and fro above her head, phallic every one. In the end, all was rubble.

She moaned and again Homer tried to take her in his arms and again she refused. Had that ever happened before? She could not remember but she did not think so. She did not want his flesh in hers. It was too dangerous: an opening she could not control. She was half asleep.

Upstairs Jason, as if responding to the tumult and upset of the night, woke and started to cry. Isabel, glad for once to be called fully into consciousness, got out of bed and went upstairs to see what was the matter. Jason was wide awake.

'I had a nasty dream,' he said.

'What about?'

'Bombs.'

'You shouldn't be so naughty through the day,' said Isabel. 'Then you wouldn't punish yourself at night. It's your dream, you know. You own it.'

She didn't think he would understand, but he seemed to. He was open and receptive; a midnight child.

'I wasn't very naughty.'

'Biting is naughty.'

'It was my birthday. Bobby took my present.'

'No. At the cinema. You bit there. A grown-up, too.'

'No, I didn't.'

40

'Daddy said you did.'

'I didn't.'

She didn't pursue the matter. His blue eyes were wide and clear. They followed her as she moved about the room. So Dandy's eyes had followed her. Every day, she thought, he grows more like Dandy. I never thought of that. I thought if the child took after anyone he would take after me. I thought that somehow you snatched a child from a man and that was that. I thought, moreover, that I would have a girl. That I would have a boy, and carry the father with me for ever and ever, was something I never envisaged.

She kissed him goodnight, settled him for sleep, and went back to bed.

'Everything all right?' asked Homer.

'Fine,' said Isabel.

3

Now. Washington's clocks are five hours behind those of London. It was seven o'clock in the evening when, on the thirty-fifth floor of the Evans building, which towers over the rushing and romantic waters of the Potomac river and houses the overflow from the Russell Senate office building, Joe (Hot Potato) Murphy and Pete (Kitten) Sikorski resolved to work late on something that had just turned up on the print-out.

Joe and Pete had semi-official access to the big CIA computer along the river. Both were ex-Company men. Now they were part of the big new up-and-coming Ivel-for-President campaign team. Their days of Dirty Tricks were past. Joe and Pete worked tirelessly and logically for the IFPC and, so far, within the law. If both kept firearms in their office drawers, and bedroom shelves, and gun holsters beneath their left arms, both were licensed and entitled so to do. They were allies; kingmakers. They were devoted and loyal. Hot Potato and Kitten! Joe and Pete made more of their nicknames than did their familiars and friends, perhaps feeling the need for sympathetic magic to make themselves ordinary and kind, and more like other men.

'Praise be,' said Joe Hot Potato Murphy, staring at the coded print-out. He liked to emphasise his Irish origins. He cultivated the twinkle in his eye and the roguish charm of his manner. They disarmed the unwary.

'Here's the Australian bitch again. She's moved up a notch to the Pay Good Attention file. What are our options here, Pete?'

Pete proposed and Joe disposed. Pete had one degree in economics and another one in law, and burn marks on his upper arms, to mark the spots where he had practised steeling himself against pain.

'We disclose nothing,' said Pete, 'in case we blow something. This is a very sensitive area.'

'It might be more sensitive than we can legitimately handle,' said Joe.

'Hell no,' said Pete. 'She's just a woman like any other.' Pete's wife was a tall, pretty blonde who sprayed herself all over with deodorants four times a day, so as not to cause offence. If she stood still, which she seldom did, so busy was she in the pursuit of hygiene and physical perfection, that she appeared like a painting against the drawing-room wall, framed by drapes. Then the sound of her husband's voice would activate her again, and her pretty hands would start patting and folding and tidying and replacing, and her long legs would scissor to and fro, and her manicured feet in their shiny shoes go clip-clip-clop on the tiled kitchen floor.

'A feminist and a radical,' warned Joe. 'And her father's a communist, now resident in Saigon. That doesn't make her a woman like any other. Her show goes out live and she's got a six-million audience hanging on her every word. And that doesn't make her like just plain folks, either.'

'We can take care of the talk show,' said Pete.

'We should have taken care of her,' said Joe, 'a long time ago.'

'Joe,' said Pete, 'quit living in the past. She's a wife and mother. We don't wage war on women.'

'It is an insult to the sweet name of womanhood,' said Joe, 'to call her a woman at all. A feminist and a radical! A wife, you say! Is a woman who makes her husband wash the dishes worthy of the name of wife? What sort of mother is it who makes her man change the baby's nappy? We have some problem with definitions here!'

'I hear you, Joe, I hear you.'

They talked like this for a while longer, using words as cloaks of darkness, the better to build the trivial into the significant; the easier to justify ill temper, neurosis and spite, and thus keep their good opinion of themselves. Now they made decisions. They would take appropriate precautionary measures, intensify the security ring around her, and wait and see how the cookie crumbled.

'There are more ways than one,' said Joe, 'of crumbling cookies.'

And they both went home to their wives, comforted by the thought of their many options, first double-locking and otherwise securing their offices, which bristled with anti-bugging devices of one kind or another.

4

Buzz-buzz! Listen to the bees! A fuchsia hedge runs along the bottom of Wincaster Row, all the way from No. 1 to No. 31. There can't be another fuchsia like it in all London. Six foot high, five foot broad, and a mass of scarlet flowers for most of the summer. What trick of soil and weather and intent produced it, I do not know.

I cannot see it now but I can hear it. The bees suck the flowers all summer long, humming and buzzing, quite overwhelmed by their discovery of such an extensive treat. I am sure they come from as far afield as Enfield, and Richmond, and Epping and Dulwich: from the green outer suburbs. For surely bees live in hives, and where in the crowded inner city is there room or time for anyone to keep beehives? Neighbours would complain.

Hilary suggested to the garden committee that the hedge be removed: she thought the bees were dangerous: she thought they might sting her little girl, Lucy. The garden committee looked at her in amazement, and explained that bees were good, and necessary to man's survival.

'What about woman?' asked Hilary, triumphant.

That was when she was pregnant for the second time, having lapsed briefly into heterosexuality with a man who could be guaranteed to treat her badly and abandon her; which indeed he did, in the sixth month of her pregnancy.

Hilary then worried, throughout the seventh and eighth months, in case the baby turned out to be male, and as such designated as enemy and rejected by the lesbian friends on whom she now depended for help and support, and who gave it gladly but not unconditionally. Hilary could not bear the thought of handing a male baby out for adoption – a Caucasian male infant, a prize in the world of baby-bargaining would be handed out to the straightest of straight middle-class couples. And then she, Hilary, would be responsible for bringing into the world she was trying to reform the worst form of male oppressor. Nor could she damage little Lucy by exposing her to the brutality and aggression of a male brother. In the ninth month the only solution seemed to be to put down the baby at birth, if it should be male. She wept and writhed and told Jennifer, and Jennifer refused to speak to her any more.

'She's wicked!' said Jennifer. 'Wicked!'

'She's mad,' was all Hope would say. 'She'll be better when the baby's born. How could anyone look like that – tight to bursting – and not be slightly mad? Let's hope it's temporary.'

And Hope waved her scarlet, perfect fingernails in the vague direction of Hilary, who refused to wear the kind of full and blousing garment which would hide her extraordinary shape – she seemed to be without fat, and the baby lay

47

inside her, with its folded form straining and outlined just beneath, it seemed, the skin of her belly.

When the baby was born, plopping easily into the world, it was, indeed, discovered to be a boy, and Hilary loved him very much, and little Lucy spent her time attending to its infant male needs; and Hilary's friends were indeed scornful of its maleness; and Hilary's lovers complained of the attention she paid it in the night; so Hilary renounced her lesbianism altogether, and thereafter had to put up with Jennifer's rather patronising forgiveness, and the told-you-so attitude of Wincaster Row.

The new baby's father, even, cautiously, came back from time to time to dandle it upon his knee. He took Lucy out as well.

'I'm not one of your sissy men,' he'd say. 'I'm not one of those poncy men who dance attendance upon feminists and get their kicks out of being mentally whipped, and run the crèches at women's conferences in return for a kick and a smile. I'm just sorry for the poor little bugger.'

Hilary would dance up and down with rage. She was a beautiful girl, in a brownish, sinewy kind of way, and tried to live by her principles. Even Jennifer acknowledged it.

'The world is so arranged,' said Jennifer, surprisingly, 'as to make doing right almost impossible. At least Hilary is trying.'

Jennifer gives Hilary little dresses and little white socks for Lucy, but Hilary just puts them in the jumble sale,

48

and Lucy goes on wearing dungarees. Lucy longs for dresses and dolls, but perhaps that is only because she isn't allowed them.

I had a baby once: it was neither male nor female. It was born without reproductive organs: it died within five minutes of birth and just as well. Extraordinary things are born to woman: mutants of another race, unviable. Cling to a sense of self through that, if you can. Of purpose. I asked the doctor not to tell Laurence what the matter with the baby was. (Can we call this thing, my child, a baby?) How could I say to Laurence, you and I together, this is what we made. Nothing. We cancelled each other out. I bore the burden of this knowledge alone. Stillborn, I said, and Laurence didn't ask any further: barely a why or a wherefore, and he an investigative journalist, and, as usual, away at the time.

Easier to find out and condemn what goes on in another country, in a far-off place, than what happens in your own home and in your own heart.

I told Isabel. 'Aren't you angry?' she asked. 'I would be, if fate picked me out amongst millions, and dealt me a blow like that.'

I replied that I had worn anger out. But it may not be so. Perhaps after all it was red rage that burned out my eyes. Or perhaps it was only fate, being kind, dealing me a trump card. Certainly I have caught Laurence's butterfly nature on the pin of my helplessness; he struggled a little and made his protest, drunk and unshaven down at the pub, and now lies still, and holds me in his arms, careful and caring and good at last, frightened to move suddenly unless something else gets torn.

You really cannot expect a blind woman to have a baby. Some do, of course, but it isn't expected. Soon I will be too old, in any case, and saved.

Buzz-buzz! How busy we all are along Wincaster Row. At least the bees stop at night, when cold slows their wings and the weight of the honey they won't let fall all but defeats them. They make it back to the hive if they can, and die if they can't, uncomplaining and dutiful. A bee could spend its days, as a butterfly does, glorifying its maker, dancing in the sun, rejoicing in the Lord – but no, it prefers to labour. Nevertheless, the bees are clearly pleased by the fuchsia hedge.

Work in Wincaster Row does not stop when night falls. Then the fuchsia bush hangs darkly and silently at the end of the garden. I remember it from my sighted days: how the lights from the windows – which sometimes burned all night – would outline its shape: it seemed then a hovering storm cloud, picked out with flecks of blood.

Oliver the architect sometimes works until two or three in the morning. He is designing a building for the disabled: he works for nothing. Anna, his wife, would prefer that he should work for something and spend more time with her and the children: but seldom says so.

'For heaven's sake,' Hope says crossly, 'if only everyone would look after themselves and forget about the rest of the world, it would be in a much better state.'

Hope's lovers bring her chocolates and flowers, in the hope of making her feel something more than kindness towards them. They puzzle her. What is it they *want*? Sex she understands, and offers, but they want her essence, her very soul, not just her body. She is writing a paper on Thucydides. No one will pay her for it, she explains. It will be published in an obscure magazine and forgotten. But it's interesting: such things must be written. Hope lectures in Greek poetry at Birkbeck College, to mature students. They study for the sake of it, not in the hope of future employment. One pupil is over eighty.

Buzz-buzz! Dawn's breaking. I can tell, because I hear the bees.

Hope once got stuck halfway up the oak tree in the communal garden. She was trying to rescue a kitten. Hope wept: the kitten wailed: the fire engine arrived. Ivor the alcoholic fell hopelessly in love with Hope, for at least a month, and Ivor's wife baked bread furiously, in the hope that her proper domestic worth and value would become apparent to him – which indeed it always was, but what has love to do with just deserts? Those who don't deserve it, receive it. Those who most need it, seldom have it. To those who hath, as Jesus once observed, to the shock and dismay of all around, shall be given, and to those who hath not, even that small portion that they hath shall be taken away.

It was Hope who let the men who called themselves electricians in to No. 3. They turned up at six one morning in a London Electricity Board van, when Homer, Isabel and Jason were off visiting friends in Wales, and spent an hour inside the house, seeing, they said, to faulty wiring.

Hope was out early trying to find a kitten she thought she heard crying. *Buzz-buzz!* She shinned up a drainpipe for the LEB men, climbed over on to the balcony, and in through the window and down to the hall, through the coats and the bicycles and by the grandfather clock, and opened the front door for them, before you could, as it were, say Jack Robinson.

'Thank you, miss,' they said, admiring. She had lovely legs, which showed to advantage as she leapt gazelle-like from point to point on the face of the building. Hope always let everyone in, up and down the row, if they'd forgotten or lost their keys.
'Think nothing of it,' she said.

No doubt they could have let themselves in more simply, had she not happened to be out of bed early, looking for a lost kitten.

After the electricians had been and gone, listeners could hear everything that went on in No. 3, if and when they wanted. The IFPC had their listening devices installed. *Buzz-buzz!*

5

Homer, for a day or so, said no more about Jason needing to see a child therapist. Isabel went nervously about her work and life, watching Jason for signs of inner disturbance. Any child, when watched closely, when faith has gone, can appear both deranged and malicious. Naïvety can seem calculated, charm self-conscious, the noisy and instant expression of emotion a covert attack upon the adult. Isabel knew this, and reassured herself. Jason was a six-year-old child behaving like a six-year-old child, and was neither her persecutor nor her victim.

Which was just as well, because if Jason was indeed suffering some inner turmoil, which only truth would resolve, then she would have to start digging away at the very foundation of her life with Homer, and this she did not wish to do. Self-interest, as well as maternal pride, was at stake. Jason, for everyone's sake, had to be in good heart and good health.

Dandy Ivel made a speech about probity, integrity, endurance and fidelity. It was reported on British television. Isabel changed programmes. Homer said, 'That man throws abstract words about like karate chops, the better to confuse and terrify.' Isabel said, 'Yes, doesn't he?'

Isabel and Homer and Jason went to stay for the weekend with the Humbles, in Wales. Ian and Doreen had given up their Wardour Street life of (him) dress-designing and (her) film-making, and taken to sheep-farming up a distant Welsh hillside. Ian and Doreen drove a battered Land Rover stuck with anti-nuclear stickers, and their children were dressed in stiff woollen garments, hand spun, natural dyed, and knitted on very thick needles; their tiny limbs, thus encased, and macrobiotically lean, found movement difficult. They sat on the splintery wooden floor of their homestead and wailed. Jason took offence at this, and no amount of reproof or explanation could prevent him from setting about them with his fists.

'Jason, they're only little. Please stop.'

'Jason, it's their home, their toys. They don't understand about sharing. They don't go to school, as you do!'

Doreen taught the children at home, as she was qualified to do. She didn't want them subjected to the brutality and corruptness of (presumably) the likes of Jason.

'Jason, if you go on like that, you'll have to go to bed.'

Jason was frightened by the dark and the silence and became hysterical when Isabel tried to put him to bed, wrapping tentacle-like limbs around hers. Presently, when he was calmer, Homer took him away and bathed him, in a tin bath in the outhouse filled by hand from a tank inadequately warmed by a solar panel. But Jason found the presence of a broody hen offensive and frightening (according to Homer, later) and then bit his father in his struggle not to be bathed, and then denied that he had, although the marks were clear enough on Homer's ankle.

'He doesn't travel well, that's all,' said Isabel, lightly, and pointed out that Ian and Doreen's girls twitched and scowled and whined; and that although they didn't make nearly so much noise as Jason, they were equally troublesome, and had stolen his silver tractor and hidden it, quite deliberately.

'But they didn't *bite*,' said Homer. His horror of biting was irrational, he agreed. A child might well feel it reasonable to use his teeth to make an impression, in every sense of the word: nevertheless, Homer was upset by it.

The night they returned to London Jason wet the bed. Homer stripped the sheets and washed and turned the mattress.
'Isabel, you must see,' he said. 'Jason is upset and worried and needs help. What are you worried by? What are you so guilty about? I don't understand it. It's so unlike you.'
'I don't want him defined as disturbed,' she said. 'I don't want him given pills.'
'Neither of those things will happen,' said Homer. 'Perhaps you're afraid of some criticism of you? That it might be said that Jason's troubles stem from your work? But we both know that isn't so: my working is as likely to upset Jason as your working. We've both been equally involved in his upbringing – except I notice it's me dealing with the sheets when he wets the bed!'

Isabel capitulated. Homer brought Dr Gregory to her attention.

'Who recommended him?'

'Colin Matthews.' Colin Matthews was one of Homer's authors. He wrote bestselling political novels.

'But you don't trust his judgement or his politics or his style. How can you trust him to be right about a child psychologist?'

'Dr Gregory saw his daughter through a bout of head-banging. Little Antonia. Do you remember? We went to her christening party.'

'We shouldn't have gone. It was hypocrisy. The whole child's life is based upon hypocrisy. The father's a fascist and the mother a hyena, and Antonia goes to a Steiner school. No wonder she banged her head.'

Isabel knew she was being unreasonable and ridiculous. She could feel her bottom lip, already so thinned and mutilated, tightening and narrowing yet more, to become, in the end, her mother's.

'Perhaps that's what Dr Gregory pointed out,' said Homer, patiently.

'She'd have probably stopped anyway,' said Isabel. 'You don't meet that many adults who bang their heads – or bite people's ankles, for that matter.'

'You do in mental homes,' observed Homer. It was the last protest Isabel made. She rang Dr Gregory. The only appointment he had available was at three the following afternoon. Isabel accepted.

She had forgotten, of course, that she would have to fetch Jason out of school before time. In so doing, she encountered Mrs Pelotti.

'Jason? Leaving school early to see a psychiatrist? You astound me. Why are you doing it? Did the recommendation come from the school? No? Then what are you doing to the child? Jason is a great trial to all of us, but he isn't disturbed. There is nothing wrong with Jason that shouldn't be wrong with all of us. Are you a cabbage? No! Is your husband a cabbage? No! Then why expect your unfortunate child to be a cabbage?'

Mrs Pelotti had a low opinion of parents, who seemed to her, from her long experience of them, to have their children's worst interests at heart. The middle classes over protected; the working classes were themselves a source of actual danger to their progeny. She took children in from the age of three – all of them, selection being by catchment area alone. She took in the backward and the brilliant, the sickly and the healthy, the mad and the sane, the poor and the rich, bullies and victims – and wherever her eye fell there was health, sanity and energy. The red-brick building, with its high echoing walls, rang to the sound of child music and was brilliant with child art, and where she trod flowers, both artificial and natural, bloomed. If her eye could not fall upon, her foot could not seek out, every corner of the school; if bullying and misery and meanness of every kind swept in with the litter off the street, blown in by winds of urban discontent, it was not her fault, nor her predecessors', nor those who would come after her, when finally she lay down exhausted and died.

Of Mrs Pelotti's pupils one out of every five came from homes where there was a mother at home and a working father. The rest had empty houses to return to; or were brought up by mother or father alone; or by grandparents or elder brothers or sisters; or by foster parents. All had roofs over their heads, and shoes, usually sneakers, on their feet; but seldom the roof they wanted, nor shoes that fitted.

Isabel and Homer sent Jason to Mrs Pelotti's school because they thought they should, and because he was happy there. Friends had children who went to schools where fees were paid and blazers worn and feet clipclopped in polished lace-up shoes, and these parents blamed Isabel and Homer for sacrificing Jason on the altar of socialist, or whatever, principle. Isabel and Homer said they didn't want Jason growing up fearful in a world in which he didn't participate. And how could society ever be changed for the better, they asked themselves and each other, if the middle classes reserved privilege for their children? Mrs Pelotti, they reasoned, needed their help.

Mrs Pelotti this morning, seemed in no need of help.

'You see,' said Isabel, 'he's taken to biting!'
'So?' said Mrs Pelotti. 'So would I if I were him. You talk to him too much. You ask his advice. You forget he's too young to give it. You treat him as if he were grown-up. He's only six. Of course he bites. He could never talk his way round you lot. What else is he to do?'
'Anything else we do wrong?' asked Isabel.
'Yes,' said Mrs Pelotti, 'you're always late. Bring him in on time and collect him on time. You and your husband spend so much time discussing whose turn it is that the child gets forgotten. But take him to a shrink if it entertains you, and you've got the money. I don't suppose it will do much harm. If you have things to throw away there's a

jumble sale next week. I have become more a fund raiser of late than an educationalist. I have no choice.'

'Mrs Pelotti,' said Isabel, surprised. 'I'm never late.'

'One of you is,' she said. 'Perhaps it's your husband. You're both so busy you never notice anything.'

That over, Isabel went to work. Mrs Pelotti had been unfair. Jason was almost always delivered and collected on time, but Mrs Pelotti's way was to brisk up both parents and children by brutal overstatement, and send them away with some kind of achievable, practical mission. If you were five you learnt to tie your shoelaces; if you were thirty-five you aspired to get up on time.

'And don't worry,' Mrs Pelotti called after her. 'There's nothing wrong with Jason. Nothing whatever.'

Isabel felt less threatened. If Dr Gregory was to be purely cosmetic, she could reassure Homer by taking Jason to see him, and reveal no confidences herself. All would yet be well.

That night, Isabel and Homer went next door to dinner, and Dandridge Ivel appeared on the television screen, pacing up and down, up and down, the weight of the world's decisions easily borne, or so it must seem to the viewer, on massive shoulders. For once, Isabel was in no position to switch him off, since Laurence was anxious, as always, to see the nine o'clock news. So she faced Dandy, instead. He stopped pacing and turned to face the camera.

He spoke, and his voice was low and powerful and precise. She thought that perhaps he had put on weight, but that it suited him. And if he was more florid than she

59

remembered, that might well be the quality of American film, as picked up by British television, and if it was more than that, was only after all what was expected in a politician. Men of affairs dined perhaps too well for their own good. The dark, intelligent eyes, with their hint of sadness, of hard lessons learned and assimilated, still flashed with knowledgeable charm; and the kind mouth curved in its sensuous way, but Isabel felt no desire, and no jealousy that his lips continued so well without her. He now seemed, to Isabel, like a painted landscape on a nursery wall, which a child once loved, but now that the child has grown can be seen for what it is, crude and inappropriate. Yet because it holds the memory of love and innocence and wonder it is better to forget it altogether: turn it to the wall. She did not want to think about him. Others clearly did. The painting turned out to be a primitive and marvellously valuable.

'The politics of confrontation are worn out,' said Dandridge Ivel. 'We have left the age of isms – capitalism, communism, socialism. We are all of one race, the human race: and we must learn to treat each other kindly. Kindness must suffuse our dealings with each other – white to black, nation to nation, state to citizen, man to woman, parent to child. We must enter a new era of compassion. I do not mean softness, or the kind of idle permissiveness which has passed for caring, but that same compassion which the father feels for the child: it includes toughness, discipline and above all, love.'

'I wonder who writes his speeches,' said Laurence, impressed.

'He does,' said Isabel, without thinking. 'Or so I read somewhere,' she added.

Dandy was engaged to be married to a girl called Pippa Dee, a tennis star and swimmer. Clips showed her to be pretty and healthy and affectionate, and to European tastes unerotic. She was of Polish descent: she had a wide peasant face made lovely by good food and healthy rearing and proper dentistry – large-eyed and snub-nosed, with high cheekbones and hollow cheeks. Dandy Ivel and Pippa Dee! It seemed laughable, in London. The very laughability of it made his eventual election more likely, all agreed. It was as if power liked to show an innocent, smiling, homely face, while it waited for its time to come, its moment to arrive.

'Jimmy Carter was laughable once,' said Homer. 'He was a peanut vendor. And Ronald Reagan the movie actor seemed a joke to many. Both, eventually, seemed deeply serious. And Pippa Dee as First Lady would enchant many. Jackie Kennedy brought French menus to the White House: Pippa Dee could bring tennis courts and swimming pools. He's on to a winner.'

'The human race faces dangers beyond its own comprehension,' said Dandridge Ivel. 'It is our duty to stir the heart and imagination of America, so that it understands these dangers, and no more wishes to annihilate than it does to be annihilated. We are in danger of seeing ourselves as a Master Race: we must come to understand that we are human beings first, and Americans second.'
'That's for the European market,' said Homer. 'They'll edit that section out, back home.'
'You're being cynical,' said Laurence, surprisingly. He who was meant to be hard-boiled.

'There is no doubt,' said the commentator, 'that Dandridge Ivel, the Senator from Maryland, orphaned son of a small-town storekeeper, who by dint of determination, energy, charm – and some even add honesty – has made his way to the top of the political tree, has a charisma all his own, and is a hot contender in the Presidential race. He seems, and looks, and feels like fresh blood, and what's more, young blood. If he can get his act together in the next few months, if he can get his own peculiar mixture of West Coast morality, East Coast canniness and Bible Belt respectability to blend together with a little more ease, if he can continue to please everyone and offend no one: and loses not an ounce of credibility on the way I think we may safely say, here is the man, at last, for all America. The unifying factor. Dandridge Ivel.'

Dandy turned his face towards the camera. He smiled. He seemed to understand his viewers. You and I, he seemed to say, have known hard times. Yet we should not let them embitter us: rather should they temper us, making us tough but flexible, like steel.
'We must forget the past,' said Dandy, to Isabel, and a thousand million others. 'Tomorrow is another day.'
Laurence switched him off.

'Thank goodness,' said Maia, apologising to her guests. 'I'm afraid Laurence has an insatiable appetite for news.'
'It is no use pretending that the outside world doesn't exist,' said Laurence. 'And forewarned is forearmed. But I must say Dandridge Ivel seems the best piece of news to come out of the USA for decades. Didn't you once interview him, Isabel, when you first came to London?'

For dinner there was boeuf Wellington and potato salad. The food, cold, had been personally delivered by Laurence's ex-mistress Helen, who worked in a delicatessen on Haverstock Hill. It came in white boxes, tied with stretched red ribbon, French style. Helen took Maia's blindness badly, feeling it was in some way her fault, for the quarrel which had blinded Maia's eyes with tears and led to her accident had centred itself on Laurence's casual infidelities, which at the time included Helen. Maia was herself anything but casual; and it was her very intensity, Homer often observed, which sent Laurence bed-hopping, lusting after frivolity rather than sexual satisfaction. But now Maia's blindness had, as it were, validated her intensity – the blind are allowed to be deadly serious – and Laurence was wholly committed to her, sexually and personally; and Helen, weighed down by Laurence's rejection and her responsibility for Maia's misfortune, toiled up the hill on Thursday evenings with peace offerings of smoked salmon and Italian sausage, and boeuf Wellington and other things easily eaten, and not messy upon the plate. Helen chose them with anxious care.

'I was supposed to interview Dandy Ivel,' corrected Isabel. 'Ages and ages ago, when he was a senator, and on a committee investigating corruption, and I had a joke job as an international correspondent. I even had a seat on Concorde booked, but I missed the plane and lost my job. I don't talk about it much. You don't, in such circumstances.' The way to lie well, Isabel knew, is to remain as near the truth as possible. At least parts of the tale will have the ring of truth.

'Perhaps Pippa Dee will turn up on your programme,' said Laurence, 'as second best!'

63

'I shouldn't think so,' said Isabel. 'Elphick steers well clear of politics.'

'That seems a waste of human endeavour, not to mention a malleable and receptive audience,' said Homer, who didn't like Elphick. 'Besides being impossible to achieve. Even the personal, these days, is political.'

'Elphick achieves it,' said Isabel. 'And who am I to quarrel with Elphick? He is my livelihood, my future and my income.'

'I thought I was supposed to be all those things,' said Homer, and everyone laughed.

'Morality must come later,' said Isabel. 'When we can afford it. Here's to Dandy Ivel and Pippa Dee!'

The following day Isabel and Homer took Jason to Dr Gregory's house. It was in the leafier part of St John's Wood. He was a tall man, with a tough yellowy skin and a face that looked rather like an eagle's, and rather like an owl's. He had a gentle manner. He inspired confidence, and spoke slowly, as if there were all the time in the world. Isabel, accustomed to the quick speech and quicker thought of her colleagues, found his slowness disconcerting. She felt he was sitting in judgement upon her: groping for ultimate truths, and not the passing ones she was used to.

'I expect he *is* sitting in judgement on you,' said Homer. 'And on me. Conventional wisdom is that the troubles of the children are always the parents' fault.'

Dr Gregory spoke to Isabel and Homer and Jason all together, and then to Jason alone, and then to Homer alone, and then to Isabel.

'What did he say to you?' asked Isabel of Jason.

'Nothing,' replied Jason.

'What did you do, then?'

'Nothing.' Jason seemed pleased with his secret, whatever it was. Isabel felt he had grown suddenly away from her: what had once been a crack was now a yawning chasm. Her child was departing from her, wrenched away; her arms were outstretched but his back was turned, in indifference. His life was starting. What did hers matter?

'What did he say to you?' asked Isabel of Homer.

'He asked me about my childhood and my sex life.'

'What did you say?'

'Nothing much. I said my parents were authoritarian and my sex life excellent.'

'Thank you.'

'Not at all.'

'My sex life?' repeated Isabel to Dr Gregory, in her session alone with him. 'What an odd phrase. It makes it sound so separate from the rest of my life.'

'Most of my patients know what I mean,' he said, smiling gently. One of his eyes wandered slightly. Sometimes it was hard to know in which direction he was looking.

'I'm not your patient,' said Isabel. 'Jason is.'

'I'm glad you make the distinction,' he said. 'Some of my mothers can't tell themselves from their children, and that leads to all kinds of trouble. What do *you* think is the matter with Jason?'

'Nothing.'

'Then you are probably right. How *is* your sex life?'

'Rotten,' said Isabel, without thinking, and having said it, thought it might well be the truth. Sex with Homer was an agreeable exercise; it neither focused nor centred their marital life, as surely lovemaking could and should. She allowed herself to remember how sex once had been, and could perhaps be again, and even as she spoke the horizons of her consciousness widened. They included now anxiety and loss and fear, but a great hope: a vision of a picture. It was as if she were eighteen again. She trembled, and thought she would cry.

'A source of trouble between you and your husband?'

'No. A source of nothing.'

'Oh. What should it be a source of?'

'More children.' Again she spoke without thinking. 'But I can't do that,' she added. 'Jason is enough to be getting on with, and Homer is an only child and so am I, and somehow I suppose it seems to both of us that one child is what a family has.'

'But you haven't talked about it to Homer.'

'No.'

'Yet you talk about most things.'

'On and on, yes. For ever.'

And we could go on like this, thought Isabel, on and on, and say everything and get nowhere. That's all right. She was her own rightful age again. Secure, and a little bossy, knowing the rules.

'I think you are holding something back,' he said. 'Something quite important. I think there is some falsehood beneath the surface of your family life and that is what Jason reacts so badly to. Perhaps it's to do with the role reversal between you and your husband —'

'It's not role reversal,' corrected Isabel, 'it's role sharing. I hope you're not going to say Jason is disturbed because his father and I share his parenting?'

'No,' he said patiently. 'But I wonder why it seems so important to both of you.'

'Christ,' said Isabel, 'it is important. How is Western society to get out of its present mess unless parenthood is shared between father and mother? How are men and women ever going to achieve equity?'

'Equity,' he replied, 'may be a red herring. The acceptance of the male as active and the female as receptive finds an echo in most societies and in most religions, including the new Eastern ones so favoured by today's young.'

'Christ!' said Isabel again, with passion, that evening. She was speaking to Homer. 'Sexist, Freudian and Yin-Yang bullshit all rolled into one. You take Jason to see him. I'm not going back.'

In the night Jason called out. Homer went up to him, while Isabel groaned. Jason had wet the bed again.

'Next thing Dr Gregory will say,' said Isabel, defeated, lacing up her sneakers, preparing to return, 'is that feminism is a symptom of a sick society. You wait.'

'Feminism is a perfectly legitimate standpoint from which a woman can view the world –' said Dr Gregory – 'Thank you very much,' said Isabel.

'But how is a male child to stand side by side with his mother and view the world as she does? His own selfish nature and his love for you are at war. Jason is a bright, imaginative child. You are handing on to him a vision of

67

the world which does not accord with the reality around him.'

'I don't think it's that,' said Isabel.

'Then what is it?'

Isabel stared stubbornly at him, and said nothing. He waited. Outside traffic murmured politely; a child's cheerful voice called goodbye. A fig tree nodded and scraped against the window: it belonged to another age and another place. Isabel could almost feel, as a physical object, the barrier in her mind which marked off her past from her present self. Passion, response, understanding were penned up behind the wall, heaving and sighing to be let out. What passed now in her for feeling was sorry simulacrum of what she once had known.

Of course she could successfully focus herself and present herself every Monday night to a million viewers. Of course she found it easy. She was, to begin with, even before she was turned into thin air by cameras, a reproduction. It was a good reproduction, of course, recognisable only to experts, the like of Dr Gregory, as not the real thing; but still a sham, a mockery, an insult to the original by virtue of its presumption.

'I may tell you next time I come,' she said. 'If I come. In any case, Jason is your patient, not me.'

'You're more interesting,' he said, and his wandering eye, the left one, suddenly focused and registered and she realised that was the one he saw through, at any rate when judging reproductions.

'The secret falsehood at the heart of every mother!' she jeered and sneered and ranted as Homer fried rump steak.

He did it cautiously, with the extractor fan switched on. Isabel behaved more rashly – charring the meat on the outside over excessive heat, and filling the kitchen with grease and fumes – so Homer these days preferred to take on the task himself. Whilst agreeing that her steak tasted better than his, he could not, he said, bear to clean the kitchen afterwards.

'Dr Gregory's so corny! Jennifer's Adrian wets the bed and he's twelve and no one takes him to some quack. They just assume he's a heavy sleeper. Jennifer's a perfect stay-at-home mother, if ever there was one, and still Adrian wets the bed.'

'Perhaps he doesn't get enough attention from his father,' said Homer. 'And *is* there a lie, Isabel? A falsehood of some kind? You're so angry I begin to feel perhaps there is.'

'There is no lie,' said Isabel. 'But I'd certainly invent one if I could, just to get a little peace.'

That night, with Homer, she faked an orgasm; something she had never done before. It saved questions. And she longed, all of a sudden, for privacy. For action, and reaction and non-reaction to go without comment, for once.

6

Pete was writing a speech for Dandy to deliver at a convention of coal-mine managers. Whether or not Dandy would deliver it, or speak off the top of his head, Pete could not be sure.

But that was Dandy, why he inspired such love and loyalty. He had integrity. If the cap didn't fit, Dandy wouldn't wear it, no matter how chilly his ears or cold the wind.

The speech was about cleanliness; about the symbolism of pit-head showers – the desirability of replacing man with machinery in the interests of human dignity; and about the labour theory of value – profit should no longer be seen in monetarist terms. True wealth was not money, but lay in the ability of man to labour, and labour well. How not to be frightened by inflation, which could be friend as well as foe.

'Sweet Jesus, cleanliness!' said Joe, smoothing out one of Pete's discarded pieces. The floor was littered with them. When Pete was in full creative flow he was prodigal with paper. 'After last night I've given up on Dandy and cleanliness. Did you see her toes?'

The night before had been disastrous. Dandy had insisted on taking everyone off to a nightclub – where, since he had to watch his weight and his blood pressure, he had no business going in the first place – had drunk too much, ignored the nice loyal girls from Party Headquarters who always tagged along, picked a fight with a waiter, and disappeared for a couple of hours with a girl from the back of the Hat Check room, who wore sandals and didn't wash her feet and on whom clearly no one had so much as run a security check. Pippa was away batting some ball about, somewhere.

'Once he's married and in the White House,' said Pete, 'he'll settle down.' They had no doubts about the future. They did not envisage defeat, loss, failure, disappointment or humiliation. They denied all negative emotions: a habit that made them powerful, and dangerous. They stretched reality to breaking point, and because they did not know how to break themselves, would break the world instead. They could murder and kill with impunity: not so much in the belief of the rightness of their cause, or even telling themselves that ends could justify means, or in their own self-interest, but simply not realising that murder was what they had done. They changed language itself to suit their purposes. If Isabel – if anyone – had to go, she would not be killed, let alone murdered; she would be liquidated, wiped out, taken out, obliterated, dealt with, with extreme prejudice. She would be a bitch, and a foreign bitch at that; she would not be a woman, and an American. Designated as not one of their own, her obliteration would cause no remorse.

Dandy referred to them as the goons, but was mistaken in thinking they were not intelligent. Pippa said she thought they were crazy, but she was wrong: they were not insane. Both Dandy and Pippa agreed, in the folly of error, that they had to have Hot Potato and Kitten around. Anyone seeking high office risked death by political assassination: thieves had to be set to catch thieves, murderers to catch would-be murderers.

'Cross the street to mail a letter,' said Dandy, 'and you risk death by automobile. The least a politician can do is look both ways.'

Pete and Joe did not discuss the matter of Isabel with Dandy. If there was one lesson everyone had learned from Watergate it was to act without waiting for proper authority, for the less proper authority knew the better.

If Liddy hadn't hired McCord in the first place, a few men would have rotted in prison, Nixon been elected for a third and even fourth term, and the nuclear clock not stood at two minutes to midnight, but somewhere respectable like ten to. Liddy, by not taking care to cover his traces, had changed the pattern of the future. The individual, in America, was still powerful.

Chatter-chatter went the telex. It was noisy, unlike the computer, which gleamed discrete red lights when it had anything to announce.

The telex referred them to the computer. Old-fashioned backups were often required for the newer technology.

'It's our Isabel again,' said Pete. 'She's in a new code. Someone's really getting concerned.'

Joe took out the code book and started work. There was no shortcut here. Some things people had to do, not machinery.

Pete paced to and fro. His wife was starting evening classes, which he saw as a minor act of marital infidelity on her part. While he was about the nation's business she surely should be about his. Tonight he would have to go home to a baby-sitter and a meal from the icebox. It seemed no proper reward for the warrior. But she had brushed up her body, and her house, all she could; now she was starting on her mind.

7

Wham. Whee. Plop. They've built a tennis court in the gardens of Wincaster Row. It's reserved for the use of residents. I expect presently Jennifer will lead me out to the court, place a racket in my hand, and inform me that someone's devised a tennis ball with a built-in whistle, especially for the blind, and here it is. Wham!

The blind have to work hard, keeping up the morale of the sighted. See, all handicaps can be overcome! Only work, strive, aspire, and achievement and renown can be ours! There is even an undercurrent of envy: at least we – the blind, the halt, the deaf – know where we are (or aren't) and know what the enemy is. Everyone is agreed what's wrong. We are allowed our fits of melancholy, bitterness, envy, grief, even petulance. But as for the rest of us, where is our cause for complaint? We have shoes on our feet, our bellies are full, we can choose our sexual partners as we want, have children or not as we will. What ails us? There is no excuse for misery, depression or suicide.

No purpose? Then find one! Up and down Wincaster Row men and women go to evening classes: improve their health, their houses, their tennis. They set themselves little goals:

74

to overcome lust or greed, or to render themselves faithful, or slim, or whatever it is they set out to do.

Wham, whee. Tennis ball against racket. Vigorous and purposeful, cutting through doubt and disillusion. That's it! Leap, attack, parry, slam! Right and wrong analysable: victory in defeat neatly distributed, parcelled out, fairly attributed. Love-forty, game, set and match. They used to play tennis only by day, but now Oliver the architect has fixed up arc lights so that play can continue by night as well. Hope could only play after work. She plays very well: long-legged and limber. Jennifer continues five months or so into her pregnancies. It is a commonplace up and down Wincaster Row that Jennifer has frightened herself into this perpetual motherhood. She sees herself as a kind of peapod, whose purpose is to split and shell out little replicas of herself. When she was young and wild and had a degree in anthropology and took a rational view of herself and the world, she took a job as a nightclub hostess the better to study the sexual nature of man and earn a living at the same time: and found it overpowering, not open to investigation at all, but on these raw and drunken levels evil.

Jennifer ran back home and married Alec, an accountant for the *Musical Express*, who already had four children, and they now have another four between them. She has abandoned her life in their favour. Hope sees it as a form of suicide. *Felo de liberis*.

Hope means never to have children, but she is young and active and does not understand the dissolution of the body, or how important it seems, as one grows older, and limbs stiffen, and hope and energy fail, to have set something

75

new and powerful and young in motion. She is too young to know that you cannot suit your own convenience for ever, without boring yourself to tears; that ambition fails, and love, and desire. That you cannot satisfactorily root yourself in the here and now, however pleasant it seems, without including for yourself a past and a future, via ancestors and descendants, part of the great dance of the generations. Nothing proceeds, alas, without sacrifice: Jennifer is Wincaster Row's sacrifice, plodding round on flat feet and ever-swelling ankles, benign, busy, self-satisfied and frequently in pain; for when she is pregnant the bones of her hips somehow spring apart, and so far have closed up again when she delivers, but who is to say what will happen next time? Will she waddle and be in pain for ever? Perhaps, in some mysterious way, Jennifer's excessive and dangerous motherhood makes up for Hope's elegant and wilful sterility?

It was Jennifer who persuaded Isabel to talk to Dr Gregory about what Homer referred to as the lie at the root of her life. 'Murder will out,' remarked Jennifer the following Saturday when Isabel took Jason round to play, 'and truth will out. Truth is the more dangerous. The art of dealing with the truth is to let it out, little by little: then you keep it under control. Otherwise enemies get hold of it, and use it against you. Speak first, or they will.'

The noise of happy children rose around her: she lay on her back on a day bed to ease the pain of her hipbones. The day bed was Georgian and riddled with worms, but the fabric was old and faded and soft and romantic. Children had brought her wild flowers, and stuck them in a jam jar, in which the remains of home-made blackberry jam could be seen. Isabel, who was worried, anxious and guilty, and perhaps over-sensitive on this account, took Jennifer's words as an omen, and decided truth must indeed out. She would confide in Dr Gregory.

'I remember saying that to her,' says Jennifer now, guiltily, to the assembled ladies of Wincaster Row. The child she expected then is eighteen months old, and she is pregnant again. 'But I was talking about being a child, and getting into trouble at school, and hiding things from my mother, not her. Oh dear!'

Wham, whee. Laurence took me to Wimbledon. He had tickets for the Centre Court. I demurred, saying others would get more benefit. But he likes to take me with him wherever and whenever he can. We like to touch each other. Since I lost my sight I have lived as I suppose a slave in a harem must have lived – by sex and for sex: that the only purpose and the only good. Forever in the dark, forever laughing at the dawn. Laurence has caught something of my languor: I pull him down into the velvet omnipresent dark. I would rather have my sight.

I found I could follow the match quite well, what with the umpire's score and the gentle crack of normally unexercised necks, turning this way and that: and the plop of the ball, and the thrang of the racket, and the swish as the ball soared through the air. I turned my head with the best of them. Left, right, left, right. Stop. All things proceed to a conclusion. Victory or defeat.

8

'Dr Gregory,' said Isabel on the telephone, 'I would like to see you for an hour or so, if you can spare the time. I do have a problem here with which I need some help, and even though I'm not convinced the solution of that problem will help Jason, it may well help me. I am sleeping badly. I go to sleep late and wake early and as I have a demanding job to do, I can see I had better get my persona in order.'

'Mrs Rust,' said Dr Gregory, 'or is it Ms Rust –'

'Ms,' said Isabel, 'or just Isabel Rust will do.'

'Let us not suppose that because there is a problem, that problem has an answer. Life is not a kind of arithmetic test, set by God. Nevertheless, I will make time to see you tomorrow.'

Isabel had rung from the Hello-Goodnight studio. She felt more confident, more ordinary and less vulnerable to alarm here than she did at home. Jason was safely at school: his friends greeted him warmly, she noticed, and he responded with a lordly calm which switched rapidly to sniffling and rolling about under the nose of Mrs Pelotti.

'I see you've brought him here on time,' observed Mrs Pelotti. 'Do stand up, Jason, the way everyone else does.' Jason stood, and regarded her from beneath a lowering brow, pouting his full lower lip, for all the world like a blond Elvis Presley.

'Now who does he remind me of?' said Mrs Pelotti.

'Me? Homer?' enquired Isabel.

'No,' said Mrs Pelotti. 'He never seems to me in the least like either of you, either in the flesh or in the spirit. I know. That rather good-looking American politician. Dandy Ivel.'

'I can't see the resemblance myself,' said Isabel.

'Don't be late collecting him,' said Mrs Pelotti, moving on to other parents, other tasks. 'It upsets him. He has his pride, you know, like royalty. He is a very unusual little boy, and I don't say that lightly. I take a special interest in him.'

9

'When I was twenty-two,' said Isabel to Dr Gregory, 'I was very tough and hard and thought I knew how to look after myself. I could ride a horse and milk a cow and shoot a snake. I had a degree in economics from Sydney university. I had trained myself, I thought, not to need a mother. I had always done without a father. I was attractive to men; and had slept with a few and rejected many. I had inadvertently witnessed a rape – an Aboriginal girl by two white cowhands, when I was twelve. I had watched my mother allow herself to be cheated out of land and money. I had decided that women friends were a waste of time, since men kept all the power and money to themselves. I was ambitious. I meant to succeed. Does this shock you?'

'It doesn't sound very nice,' said Dr Gregory cautiously. 'But not yet particularly dangerous. I meet many young women like this.'

'I slept with my tutor at university,' said Isabel. 'That's how I got my degree.'

'No,' he said. 'That's how you would like to have got your degree. I have no doubt you got it on merit, and through hard work, like anyone else. I know quite a number of professors, lecturers, and so on. They tend to sleep with the bright students, so there can be no conflict of interest.'

Isabel found herself crying a little, she was not sure why.

'Well?' he said presently.

'I'd never been in love with anyone,' she said. 'I thought I was different from other people. There was something missing. All the other girls were in love with the tutor, except me. I could see it was rather a waste. I just thought it might be useful.'

'Yes.'

'I have rather a funny face. You may have noticed. A horse kicked it. A blow from fate. I used to think men slept with me out of pity, or because they were kinky. Look. I've told all this to Homer, there's nothing new: why does it make me cry? I have a television appearance tomorrow night. What will happen if I haven't stopped crying by then?'

'What strange new trials the human race invents for itself,' observed Dr Gregory, which irritated her and stopped her tears.

'When I was twenty-two,' she continued presently, 'I flew to England determined to make good in journalism. I took my folio with me, and I left two hundred pounds behind in debts I had incurred knowing I would never pay them. I don't know why I did that. Perhaps to ensure I would never return. I looked quite good, in spite of my face. I'd developed a kind of walk, springy from the hip, which made people look after me. I can create pretty much the impression I want on other people.'

'That is your misfortune.'

'I took elocution lessons before I left, to get rid of my Australian accent. That seemed just about the lowest thing I ever did. I've never even told Homer that. The final denial

81

of my father, I suppose. I believe he got involved in politics in North Vietnam.'

'You're not political?'

'Not in the same sense. Jesus, no. Men's games.'

'I see.' He sounded offended.

'It was a long, terrible journey. We stopped off at Singapore. There was some kind of trouble with the engine. Rumour had it we sucked in a seagull. Qantas put us up for the night at a rather good hotel. I slept with one of the First-Class passengers. Look, I was frightened – there'd been a lot of turbulence, not to mention the seagull. I was glad to be alive. We all were. He paid the extras and I travelled First Class the rest of the way. That must have put him back a thousand quid or more. You don't feel so unsafe when you travel First Class. You can't believe any of the others are going to die. When you travel Economy it seems all too likely all of them are. He was a nice man.'

'What do you mean by a nice man?'

'I mean he gave a lot in return for very little. He wished me well and looked after me.'

'As a father might.'

'I daresay.' It was her turn to sniff and look offended. She did not care for this connection between the erotic and the paternal. It devalued both.

'When we arrived at Heathrow his wife was there to meet him, so that was that, whatever he represented. He gave me a few useful names and addresses, and made a few telephone calls, by virtue of which I was spared Earls Court and the company of Australian travelling folk and their shoestring economy, and presently found myself as the resident inamorata of an industrialist, an ageing whizz kid in the electronic games business. Men of that kind pass girls on, you know. They're forever doing each other favours.

82

They like to share the good things of life, whilst making sure the less privileged don't get a look in. They're the same sexually as they are financially. Capitalist to the core. They hand around the wives too. Lady this becomes Lady that; OK. But if she runs off with the gardener, that's the end of her.'

'So you look forward to the revolution?'

'Of course. But the old system suited me, at the time. I became upset because though I shared his bed I didn't share his board. If he gave dinner parties I had to keep out of sight. He took other girls to the theatre and Glyndebourne and so on. I knew that I was more intelligent, better educated, better looking and sexier than the others. But I didn't count. He was ashamed of me. I was real life; they were aspiration. I was attainable, within reach; they just out of reach, never really gained. They might be kind, and allow the male entry into their ladylike bodies, in return for a diamond ring and the right kind of boots to shop in at Harrods, but never irrationally, the way I did, out of desire and necessity mixed.'

'Neurotic need, in other words.'

'Really? I just thought I was getting on in the world, sleeping my way to the top. Except that I was being elbowed sideways by these other cool bitches, in their horsy headscarves and tweed skirts, who came to his dinner parties in little black dresses I wouldn't be seen dead in, and I didn't understand it. But then I did get a job, on the gossip column of the *Star*. In return for selling a little scandal I was allowed to write a paragraph or two; which eventually became the whole column; for what was difficult for them – the stringing of words together – was easy for me. From there I moved sideways into subbing, and because I was generally intelligent and had read a few books and had my degree in economics and my tutor had written poetry, could at least sort news items out into their proper contexts. By the time I was twenty-three I was going really very well. People moved over for me at El Vino's. And still I wasn't asked to dinner in my own home. So I moved out. It broke my heart to have to pay rent – I had the true Australian's dislike of spending unnecessary money. If I could get someone else to pick up the tab, I would: and if they were mad at me as a result, what could it matter? I'd have moved on, would never see them again. I hadn't realised, of course, how small the world is, how few the people in it: how we move on separate but interconnecting tracks, like circuits on Jason's model railway. We never really get away with anything; passing and crossing and waving for ever. Jason's too young for the railway, of course, but Homer loves it. Homer behaves like a cliché father in an American comic strip, I sometimes think.

'Anyway, there I was in my own pad, self-supporting and self-reliant at last. I thought Daring Dan the Silicon Man would come after me, but he didn't. He married Melinda instead. She really was called Melinda, and had parents to prove it – many of those girls don't, as I discovered in my gossip column days – and all I was was a broken spring or two in his mattress. And why not? I got as much pleasure as he did, and free board and lodging beside, and I wouldn't have married him if he'd asked me. I didn't love him. Why expect him to love me? Daring Dan went bankrupt in 1976, and Melinda divorced him and married a title. That's allowed. Perhaps she was just better at whoring than me? Or perhaps she concentrated, and I didn't; or perhaps seeing the wideness of the world, as I did even then, inhibits one in one's ability to deal with it?

'In any case, at twenty-three I regarded myself as both immoral and unlucky. Some inner little regarded part of myself, what's more, kept nagging away at me, and insisting, in spite of all material evidence to the contrary, that only good actions bring about worthy results, and that the bad are punished here on earth, and not only in heaven.

'I had become a proper political correspondent – only a paper like the *Star*, I daresay, could seriously consider someone like me fit to undertake such a task, but there it was. I shared the job with a grizzled newshound of the old school – he was rumoured to have accidentally betrayed Che Guevara to the authorities and single-handedly deflated the entire world revolution: Fleet Street is nothing if not dedicated to the conspiracy theory of history, and the notion that it is great men and not great forces, individual events and not mighty sweeps of trivia, that change the order of society. I shared an office and on occasion a bed with this hero – from necessity, usually, and not choice, inasmuch as the *Star*'s management liked to do things on the cheap, and in the crowded hotels where newsmen, and a few newswomen, gathered, we thought ourselves lucky to be allocated one room, let alone two. And sleeping together involved less mental effort and general embarrassment and lengthy conversation than sleeping apart.

'Love? As I say, I thought that was something which happened to other people. I experienced rejection, humiliation, shame and all the emotions that go with unrequited love, slighted affection, but none of the positive symptoms other women had – the bright eyes, submissive glance, heightened complexion and general entrancement, accompanied by sighs and giggles, which typify the state.

85

'Sex? Again, it seemed pleasant enough, and certainly useful, and a means to getting on in the world. I slept with married men without shame, or guilt, and feeling no jealousy myself could not understand why other women could, or would. Sexual possessiveness, I maintained, in all the strength and glory of my unaware and callous youth, was old-fashioned and ridiculous, if not exactly criminal. We must all, I thought, be free. Especially me.

'I had nothing to lose, but did not know it. I daresay most people get through their lives like that.

'Now it happened one day that I was sharing a room in Edinburgh with the newshound, but not a bed, since he had a migraine; we were covering some boring question of Home Rule for Scotland. The telephone went: it was the *Star*. They wanted Gerry. It was Concorde's maiden flight the following day and they asked him to cover it: there had been rumour of plots by other airlines, if not to sabotage the aircraft itself, certainly to scuttle its hopes of economic survival.

'"Gerry's gone up North: he's in the Highlands somewhere uncovering a bomb-making factory. I can't get hold of him," I said. Gerry lay on the bed in the darkened room, listening to my lies. He did not groan, or complain. He had an old bullet wound in his leg, from Korea, and a white streak across his forehead where a Vietnamese bullet had glanced: men like that do not groan. They lie, and wait, in silence. If he had wanted to protest he could have. He said nothing: he let me lie.

'I wanted to go to Washington. I wanted to go abroad. I wanted to go on Concorde's maiden flight. Gerry was fading and sinking and I was rising, bright and fierce. But I think, really, he just could not be bothered with me. My ambition, to him, must have seemed pitiful, the lie ridiculous. It does to me now, too. I am embarrassed to think of it. I know now you cannot sleep or lie or scratch or stab or betray your way to the top: there is, in the end, only self-esteem.

'I took the shuttle flight down from Edinburgh to Heath-row. We were delayed by fog. When I emerged into Terminal One loudspeakers were calling my name: a truck waited for me, and rattled me round to Terminal Three and Concorde, and I ran on board, with the heel of my shoe broken. I think they call it "emplaned". I missed the champagne and the canapés.'

'What are you trying to tell me?' asked Dr Gregory. 'That you are not the woman you seem? That this is what Jason reacts to? If that is all, you need not go on. Truth is a funny thing. Layers must be peeled and peeled away: once you start you cannot go back. Sometimes it is better not to start, but put up with things as they are. There is no guarantee that truth will bring happiness or peace of mind. It can be dangerous. It is not even something definable. It is more a mountain, that the knowing try to climb.'

'I shall go on,' said Isabel.

Dr Gregory, for some reason, sighed.

10

Well. *Cris de joie*. '*Défense d'émettre cris de joie*' as the French sometimes command, on little notices in hotel bedrooms up and down the land. Do not disturb the rest of the world; do not remind the unsatisfied that satisfaction exists. Let us not draw attention to the wildness, the uncontrollability, of man's animal nature. In man, of course, we include women – the *cris de joie* uttered by the female are stranger and more alarming than those drawn out of man.

I hear them up and down Wincaster Row, with my new fine ears: they are muffled by bricks and mortar and curtains and carpets, but I hear them all the same, or think I do.

Isabel's cries, with Homer, were gentle and polite. I heard them.

I do not think the subject is particularly tasteful. Hope and Jennifer and Hilary look disconcerted now when I bring it up. We all like to think we have things more or less under control; and when we haven't, that other people won't be listening.

But if we are to understand Isabel's story, which I now

report to them as she reported to me, and with her permission so to do – indeed, her lordly command that I do so – I think I am entitled to my discursions into the nature of our life and times.

Cris de joie. Since I lost my sight and gained my husband the world seems to ring with them. They are not good or bad: they are there all around. When I had eyes, I never heard them. 'And the valleys shall ring to Thy Praise, O Lord.' What else could the psalmist have meant? The bleating of sheep on the yellowy Mesopotamian hills? No. I think he too heard the *cris de joie*, which almost, but not quite, blot out the tears of misery and fear which follow them.

11

Picture it, then. Concorde, the great white taloned bird of myth and legend, wheeled out on to the tarmac. Around it gathered newsmen and airline officials and captains of airspace industry, public relations men, photographers and film-makers. All thought, as it were, that the bird was their special pigeon, and could not understand the presence of the others. The passengers were assembled in the newly-constructed Concorde lounge, sipping and nibbling, and concealing their fear (in most cases): and (in a few) their honest excitement. Women had had their hair done and men wore new suits, to fit the new age of supersonic flying and salute the achievement of the British Aircraft Industry. The French claimed a share in it but this was largely ignored. The sun shone, the sky was glazed: everyone was too hot, and carefully groomed faces turned pink and sweated.

Amongst the passengers was Dandy Ivel, the Senator from Maryland, youngest member of the US Senate for twenty-two years. He had been making a special study of Anglo-French military relations since World War II, and had found time for a pilgrimage to the House of Lords library, to study the Joe Kennedy/Beaverbrook letters lodged there. Now he was on his way home.

Sitting in the First-Class Pan Am lounge, barred from the Concorde flight, were Joe Murphy and Pete Sikorski. They had been with Dandy for three months, and were on the payroll of the still undercover Ivel-for-President Campaign Committee. Even Dandy scarcely knew of its existence: it was composed of racehorse owners, businessmen, politicians, lawyers and accountants, united in the idea that Dandy was the man they wanted for President. Not the only possible, or the least undesirable, or the hopefully electable – but an actual positive, moral and cheerful *want* – that Dandy should be President. Dandy had charisma. Where Dandy went, eyes followed.

Dandy was the kind of man that young men wanted their fathers to be, and old men wanted their sons to be. Well-built, evangelistic, responsible, intelligent, heady, honest and – simply – good to be with. Devious when he had to be, but not otherwise. A certain lack of guile, a certain rashness, a certain wilfulness, perhaps – but were not these the marks of a leader?

These things had been put to Pete and Joe by Harry McSwain of the IFPC. A Presidential Candidate, he said, had to present himself like a handkerchief, freshly laundered: turn over any layer, and it must appear fresh and clean. The Security Agencies of the United States, he said, had the best surveillance techniques in the world: they could, and would, throw up dirt on anyone, even the Pope. Pete and Joe must just see that it wasn't the kind of dirt that stuck, or did damage. Pete and Joe were experienced agents, they would know what to do. Pete, after all, had worked for the Bureau in the last mad days of Hoover – Joe was ex-CIA. Both were members of the anti-gun law lobby. What their exact function was in relation to Dandy would not be made clear: it would be left to them. That was the way Dandy's back-up organisation worked. It chose its members carefully, and after that the initiative lay with them. Men of good character and good intent must surely be left to make their own decisions?

'You are kingmakers,' Harry McSwain had said, looking out on to the beauty of rolling hills and wild sky that he and his like could afford to own and keep for themselves. 'That is all you must remember. It is a great task. We are all kingmakers. The people of Israel came to the prophet Samuel and said "Make us a king" and so he did; men think they want presidents, but in truth they want kings. It's all in the Bible. So be it.'

And that was the end of it. Pete and Joe tucked their holsters more firmly under their armpits and settled down to business, creating for themselves, by dint of finding danger wherever they looked, a whole new world of challenge and occupation. Dandy himself eyed them with mixed respect and mirth. They were useful: they carried bags, provided cash, made hotel bookings, fed his speeches through computers to check out their acceptability, provided rapid résumés of places and people, checked out the nutters, and proofread articles. They took his shirts to the laundry and found his shoes. They tried to stand between him and women and drink, and failed.

Dandy was to be eight hours out of Pete and Joe's sight. Their Pan Am flight left four hours later than his: Concorde would take half their time to make the journey. The thought made them uneasy.

'Have some more white on the rocks,' said Joe. 'Relax. What's the hassle?'

'They aren't rocks,' complained Pete. 'They're goddamned pebbles.'

He had had a painful argument with the drinks waiter, who had officiously pointed out that Veuve Clicquot did not need ice. The waiter was upset because Concorde had creamed off his best customers and left the dross.

'Christ!' said Pete, proving his point, 'who cares what the drink needs? It's what I need that matters. I pay. The drink just gets to be drunk. This country is full of crazy people.' He'd won, of course, but was as humiliated as the waiter intended, and thereafter attended to British affairs with especial severity. Joe had never liked the British. His mother came from Dublin. One of his uncles had been killed by the Brits, and two of his great-uncles. Now, beneath them, Concorde rolled into place. The passengers embarked. Pete and Joe caught a glimpse of Dandy.

'He can't get into much trouble crossing the Atlantic,' said Pete.

'Mick Jagger did,' said Joe, 'and the whole world knows it.'

'That was a Jumbo. The seating on Concorde's too narrow,' said Pete. 'It's on a two-two design. And we've checked out the passenger list. And Harry McSwain's meeting him at Dulles.'

'Poor bastard,' said Joe, meaning Dandy. He imagined Dandy feared poetry as much as he himself did, and was wrong.

'Last call for Concorde's maiden flight to Washington,' said the tannoy. 'Last call for Miss Isabel Rust. Will Miss Isabel Rust go at once to Gateway eleven.'

Pete and Joe were not happy. Miss Isabel Rust was not on their final passenger list, which had been issued only the day before. Someone, someone female and unknown, soon to be cooped up for four hours with Dandy, unsupervised, was late, was acting out of line. It was the way trouble started. They had a nose for it.

Isabel boarded. They had a glimpse of reddish hair, slim calf in tight jeans. It was not reassuring.

Picture it, then. Film whirring, cameras clicking, people cheering. Concorde rises into the air by magic and is off. Its noise is left behind. It has no truck with it. In the Pan Am First-Class lounge two men stand, glasses in hand, staring after the departing bird. They are well-suited and well-shod; well-shaven and manicured. They have no money worries. They are both happily married to faithful, hardworking wives. Pete has a broad brow and a narrow jaw, and hollow cheeks. He is tall and thin, and stooping. His grandparents came from Poland. Joe is squatter and swarthier: his eyebrows beetle; his black pupils glitter. His Irish mother married, in California, a man who was partly red Indian.

Concorde disappears in a cloud of black mist, carrying Dandy and Isabel. Dandy's maternal grandfather was a White Russian prince, and his paternal great-grandfather was Sicilian. Isabel's mother was English and her maternal grandparents Celts: her father was Australian, of Viking descent, now living in North Vietnam.

How has anyone ever understood anyone, except through love, which is wordless?

Pete and Joe found the firearms they carried in their armpits reassuring. Joe's gun had been given him for Christmas by his wife.

'The best insurance policy I can give you,' she had said. He had not used it yet, but no doubt the time would come. Joe's jacket coat was weighted at the hem with shot, so that when he took aim it would swing back gracefully – as will a bull-fighter's cloak, which is weighted with sand – and not muffle his intention. His wife had sewn it in for him, lovingly. She did not have the beauty of Pete's wife, but she cooked and sewed and did not go to evening classes. She left the thinking to Joe.

12

'Ah, Dr Gregory, what can I tell you about love? You sit there in your grey suit with your pale eyes staring; the fig tree rubs against the windowpane. You wait, and the world waits. Do you understand? Do these passions overwhelm you, too, and illuminate your existence? Do you sometimes rise from your chair, and pace the room when you are left for once with your own existence, and does your breath rasp your chest with pain, just where your heart is, at the very memory of it? Your body does not seem fit to contain such glory: the hands lie pale and still upon the desk, desiccated, as if all life had been sucked from them. Yet this perhaps is what love does, or the memory of it; it sucks the life from the living, glorying body and leaves it, when love has gone, a shred, a simulacrum – dross, to be swept up from the factory floor, pitiful and dusty, useless. You are its victim, too.

No, I do not love you any more. And there you are! The scrapings from some rich, rich dinner; fit only for the dogs. Swallow, gulp and gone.

Do all men and women feel love before they die? This force, this source of light, that lies behind the sun; glances off mountains and lakes; comes upon you suddenly, glinting through the art gallery window, blinding and dazzling, on a Sunday afternoon; so brilliant you have to guard your soul, fold your arms to shield your heart from the very memory of it.

I sat next to Dandy. The hostess buckled me in. She was dressed in red, white and blue, and cross with me, because I had taken Concorde's maiden flight lightly and held everyone up. She took her own seat. We rattled off across the tarmac – so light a plane must rattle, it seems – and the air grew stiff with terror, as we poor huddling wretches, in our minks and solid gold tiepins, realised our flimsy, fleshly state: too late, too late! Oh God forgive us! We hurled ourselves into the air, in defiance of our maker. Surely like Icarus, presumptuous of our power, we would catch fire and burn, and brilliant pieces be tossed into the air, and vanish into the electric blue? And serve us right.

Dandy looked out of the window. I looked at the line of his head to his shoulder, the muscle beneath the skin, and my heart turned over with desire. Was it merely the flight from terror, Dr Gregory? Do people fall in love, just like that, on supersonic flights? No, I don't think so. When the Qantas jet sucked in a seagull I fell into bed, but not in love. I had been falling into beds ever since. Now, looking at the muscles move beneath Dandy's golden skin, I knew that that was over; that if I lived all things would be different.

Dandy turned and looked at me. He seemed to have been expecting me. He did not smile at me, and I did not smile at him. I think he even frowned a little. The occasion was amazing. The force with which we hurtled skyward gave us both sufficient cause to stare at each other, as human beings, for mere reassurance, for the simple recognition that something astonishing was, indeed, happening. But we looked at each other as man and woman, as lovers. His eyes were brown. Mine, as you may have noticed, are blue. Have you noticed?

Once you have felt love you look at people in a different way. You do not feel competitive any more: you do not believe you will be loved, or not loved, because your make-up is right or wrong. You do not worry because your breasts are small, or your hair greasy; you do not condemn other women; you stop saying why doesn't this one diet, or that one wash more often. You know that all these things are trivial, that love strikes in spite of them; and some women are lucky in love, and some aren't.

Lucky at cards, unlucky at love.

We played cards, Dandy and I, with the special pack handed out by the red, white and blue hostess. She kept handing us little gifts, in genuine leather or genuine vellum or genuine gold, and food came on genuine wooden trays with genuine silver cutlery; and it was genuine steak all right, and genuine claret, and we hurtled insanely through the air, and the earth curved away beneath us. Oh, we were genuine enough. I won at cards. He lost.

Love! Dandy took my hand. He knew I would let him, that I would not move it away. He held it as if he wanted to learn it, and I knew his touch already, and I swear that if we had been anywhere else but strapped into our seats with the booster engines going and the cabin Machmeter creeping upwards, we would have enfolded each other, and made love there and then, simply to discover whether the skin inside was the same as the skin outside. Because clearly the most amazing thing had happened: by some chance – no, the lover does not believe in chance, but destiny – destiny had arranged it so that the man and woman who had made the original whole, then somehow divided and separated by an angry God, had met up again, and now must reform the rightful, righteous whole. At once!

Lovers feel that God, in reuniting them, has made a proper apology for having in the first place brought about their separation.

I suppose we talked. Of course we talked. I knew who he was. I wanted to know all about him. He did not want to know much about me. A woman in love wants to own her partner's past, the better to protect him from the sheer evident unhappiness of his life without her. A man in love prefers his partner's life to have started the day he met her. That at any rate has been my experience.

All kinds of men, mind you, have said they loved me, and not meant it. In the extreme of sexual animation, of course, it is easily said, and easily forgiven, and easily forgotten. Otherwise it is too often used as an act of aggression. It demands gratitude: Wow! You, wonderful you, loves worthless me? Oh, thank you. Yes, I love you too. Have another drink. When a man says he loves me, I know I am supposed to shudder with wonder at the impact of his ego on mine: but love, usually, is simply not there. He has read a book or two, or dreamt a dream or two in which I

99

figured, and found a word, the wrong word, to describe the longing that the self feels, painfully enough, when it attaches itself weakly and meanly, to another. Anyone will do. That is not what I mean by love. Dr Gregory, you are tapping your pencil, you are taking notes. Does this mean I am mad? Does that mean I am an unfit mother for Jason? Because I loved, knew love, once had the capacity to love? Believe me, it is all in the past.

The children of lovers have no parents? I know. My son is orphaned. Poor Jason.

I am sorry to cry. Be patient.

Dandy and I stepped off the plane. It landed like a great bird of prey. It alighted gracefully. It had spread around great shocks of sound, and belched out an amazing volume of black smoke and left them all behind, for others to deal with, like some pretty, vicious, wilful girl stepping out of her smelly knickers, leaving them for the maid to pick up. Crowds gathered round; photographers snapped; people made speeches. Dandy held my hand tucked under his arm, for all the world to see.

Dandy and I saw a friendly, rich, pliable sort of red-faced American approaching, with a smile on his face. I'll swear he had a Bible tucked under his arm, but Dandy said no, that was just a psychic vision induced by Concorde, fear and falling in love. It was Harry McSwain, a politician friend of his, and though he was a great believer in the Bible as poetry, and often quoted from it, he did not actually carry one about with him.

Dandy smiled back, and even as he smiled ducked like a naughty schoolboy, and pulling me after him ran through all the barriers that nations put in the way of free and happy travel; and the barriers fell aside. Well, he was recognised; they waved me on, with him. Poor Harry McSwain, laughing, trying to see the joke, but failing, followed, and failed at that as well.

We took a taxi to a big hotel. They knew him there too. I waited by the gold-laced electronic doors: the lobby staff looked me up and down. I did not care. I had not combed my hair for nights and days – I had no comb. I wore, I think, jeans and a T-shirt. No, I know that is what I wore. I keep the T-shirt still, at the back of my wardrobe; it lies crumpled in a thin, greyish heap. When I die I expect someone will throw it out, wondering what the rag is doing there, what kind of slut I was.

Dandy beckoned me; we went up to room eight hundred and eleven. It was a suite: bedrooms led out of drawing rooms and into bathrooms. Everything was pink and gold, and fur and velvet: windows looked down on the White House and across to Capitol Hill. The sun shone: the sky was blue-mazed behind the glass. We had cracked the sky, Dandy and I: pierced it and riven it and conquered it. Like Lois Lane and Superman, risen through the infinite to the sound of celestial chords, we had danced to the music of time.

We lay together on the bed. He'd pulled the curtains, because the light hurt.
"We don't have to do this," he said. "It isn't necessary. Next week, next month will do."
"I'd rather now," I said, and his teeth nipped my nipples,

and I cried out, not from the pain of it, or the joy of it, but the love of it, of him.

To be an object of worship is a strange and frightening thing: to be acknowledged as the Ark itself: the shrine in which is concentrated all power, and all glory: the very fountain of love and life. I stood unclothed and the Senator from Maryland bowed down before me and worshipped me, and with infinite seriousness and reverence penetrated me, and once he had, plunged, and ploughed, and ravaged and explored, as if he would own God through me, seek out and understand the very corners of His kingdom, over-turning and scattering as he went; he was Lucifer, victori-ous, discovering his vanquished Lord's possessions, the better to rule over Him. He was violence, certainty, power and the promise of everlasting peace.

As for me, I was no longer a scheming little slut from Aussieland: no, I inhabited lands of glory, I shared the grandeur of the divine, I was elevated to the Throne of Grace; and all the possessions of the flesh, and of the spirit, all worldly and temporal power, were mine, ours.

I lay upon a bed, in an hotel in Georgetown, Washington, and he on top of me, inside me, and in the flesh, united, lay an infinite kingdom where we could live for ever.

Kings, of course, tend to keep their thrones: the same stern, wise eyes look down upon passing generations of the faithful. The face of the queen changes rather more often, in the kingdom of heaven as well as here on earth. She wears out her welcome. Off with her head!

But that was to come. In the meantime I took into my being, by osmosis, something of the dignity and power that was invested in my Dandy, their Dandridge Ivel, both by virtue of some accident of his birth, some graceful combination of genes, and the very force of America's expectation of their Senator, which elevated him and made him more, I do believe, even then, than mortal man. I understood through Dandy that the flesh as well as the soul is grace: that the body has its own mysticism; that even in sexual degradation the twisting of the body on the horrific pin of perverse desires – is purification. He swept away the memory, the obscure traces of those other men, who had gone before him inside me, and made me what I am today; not worn-away, eroded by experience, but gaining body, attracting energy with every single thing that happens to me. He made me what my mother alone could not – he made me whole.

All this I owe to Dandy. I learned that the entry of the male body into the female is a sacrament, an offering, a concentration of everything good and aspiring and great in the male, that it should so incline towards the female – the male all giving, the female all receptive.

I learned that sex was not a question of victory or defeat, of pleasure or profit: of a hand's manipulation and a physical response: I learned that in its purest pleasure it belongs to neither of those who practise it, in the same way as a child belongs to neither parent: it is a free spirit: it simply exists.

So that was how it was. Dandy bowed down and worshipped, and I obligingly took on the lineaments of the divine. To McSwain, Pete and Joe, of course, it was obvious enough that I was a false God: a graven image; a lesser version of a true form. But for a time we both, Dandy and myself, believed in my divinity: that I was indeed the Spirit made Flesh.

How can other things compare to this? Twenty days of this, of love, are worth twenty years of the leftover life that follows. I do not know how such obsession tails away into everyday life, or if it ever does. It is like the trail of an aeroplane, high above, the narrow purposeful line widening as it's left behind, as time and distance part it further and further from its source, dispersing into nothingness. I do not think I could live in the intensity, in the full blast, of love: I would not have the courage. I would rather live with Homer.

It was a kind of sweaty sickness; it was a mutual madness, thinking that the soul shone from out behind the eye, and that the spirit demanded to intertwine, and that the heaving and racking and slobbering of the body was an expression of the divinity that suffuses all things: the seas, the mountains, the heavens. Perhaps he was right: we should just have sat and held hands.

I tell you, in the end he could just touch my little finger and my whole body would convulse, not just with desire but with the satisfaction of it.

Of course there were troubles and difficulties. Harry McSwain paced up and down the corridors of the eighth floor, and Joe and Pete arrived, and let him in, and stationed themselves in the pinker of the two drawing-rooms, and lived there too, playing cards and smoking. I thought they were his friends. I thought, well, Dandy is American; I just don't understand his culture. And he is a politician; I expect that makes a difference. He had to go out from time to time, to make a speech or record a vote.

I thought that Dandy was very, very clever. I thought he was honest, too. I was surprised. I was a journalist, after all, and journalists have a poor opinion of politicians. That is not because they get to know them more intimately than other people can, but because, being journalists, they too regard the world and its suffering as fodder for their own advancement. They cannot, for the most part, understand idealism or humanitarianism, or the genuine desire to serve the body politic; the craving, simply, to make the world a better place. If they suspect it exists they will dig the knife in right to the core of the apple, and twist and turn it, spoiling the pure white flesh, until the worm is discovered.

I think I confused Dandy. I did not behave like the girls he was accustomed to. I was neither slut nor lady. I did not ask for things – money, or furs, or declarations of intent. I did not complain. I was foreign. I was nothing known: just female body, and soul, and he hurt when I was not with him, as I fainted and failed when he was not with me.

But I couldn't live there for ever, could I?'

13

Pete had run a contact check. It was closing the stable door after the horse had bolted, but it was better than doing nothing, sitting there listening to Dandy in the next room, throwing away the hopes and resources of the Ivel-for-President Committee with every lusty heave.

He was half turned-on himself most of the time; he couldn't meet Joe's eye. They slapped the cards on the table and tried to see the episode in a broader context.

Harry McSwain, over in the Evans building, read them extracts from the Song of Solomon and didn't seem too bothered. Joe tried to explain.
'The mother's OK. She lives in a sandpit in Western Australia, with a couple of mangey horses. But the father looks like real trouble. We're following it up now. The girl herself is a small-time journalist for a crummy newspaper. But she's been shacked up with Gerry Grimble; he's a drunk – old enough to be her father. He was in the big time once: all kinds of contacts there, with left-wing radicals – big ones, too. I don't like the look of this, sir. Frankly, there's a possibility she's been sent in: an agent.'

'Until the day breaks and the shadows flee,' said Harry McSwain, 'I will get me to the mountain of myrrh, and to the hill of frankincense.'

'Paranoia,' said Dandy, informed and angry; bleary-eyed with sex and lack of sleep. 'You guys don't have enough to do. Why don't you go home to your wives and take it out on them? In the meantime, get the hell out of here!'

Agents from foreign superpowers did not go without combs, observed Dandy, or with their toenails unpainted. Pete and Joe refrained from saying they probably did, if they knew Dandy's tastes.

Harry McSwain, contaminated by so much sexual and romantic energy, had abandoned the Bible and taken to Tennyson. He quoted from 'Maud'.

> *'And ah for a man to arise in me,*
> *That the man I am may cease to be!'*

'Sir, the father shacked up with a Malaysian girl! A communist sympathiser way back in World War II, and politically active, sir. He now lives in Saigon, sir.'

> *'There is none like her, none.*
> *Nor will be when our summers have deceased,'*

gloried Harry McSwain.

Like many politicians, he was a failed writer. He had taken five years out of his career, as a young man, to try to make it as a poet, and failed. He had faced parental and social disapproval, and been humiliated. They had been right. He was a man of action, not of words. Now, when times were difficult, and great moments approached, and he felt his mind quailing under the weight of responsibility, he read the Bible, or Tennyson, and found peace and conviction in the beauty of language, and exultation in Victorian sentiment.

The sun set over the Potomac: a long avenue cut the sward and led down to the Kennedy graves, where the faithful and the trusting still gathered round, bowed their living heads under black shrouds, fingered beads, and shuffled, murmuring their gentle prayers for forgiveness, blessing and peace. He wished Tennyson had been living at this hour.

'Sir,' said Joe and Pete, 'it can't go on. For all we know she's taping and recording everything.'

> *'Queen rose of the rosebud garden of girls,'* said Harry
>   McSwain,
>   *'Come hither, the dances are done,*
> *In gloss of satin and glimmer of pearls,*
>   *Queen lily and rose in one;*
> *Shine out, little head, sunning over with curls,*
>   *To the flowers, and be their sun.'*

'Sir,' said Pete and Joe, 'you've seen her. She's not like that, little heads and curly-whadd ya' mean!'
'Dandy thinks she is,' said Harry McSwain.
'Sir,' said Pete and Joe, 'can you see her in the White House? Can you see her as First Lady?'

'Who's talking about marriage?' asked Harry.

'Dandy is,' said Pete.

'I'll speak to him,' said Harry, putting down his book.

14

'The transition from that state of grace – from love to the absence of love, from trust to fear – was rapid. Once doubt has crept in, Dr Gregory, the whole structure of self belief is easily washed away. What you thought was a castle, permanent and grand, with its turrets and flags and trumpets, overseeing the landscape as far as the eye can see, turns out to be made of sand, built upon a beach, a child's fantasy; nothing but an experiment in existence, its whole purpose its eventual destruction. Once the first wave has penetrated the moat, surged nobly round from front to back, then the time is very short. Soon the beach will be flat again, and the tide, receding, wash over smooth sand. Yet once it was there, and glorious, Dr Gregory. I cannot believe the beach is not altered somehow. I will not believe it.

Why did he stop loving me? Can you tell me that? I can better understand why people fall in love than why they fall out of it. The madness is more comprehensible than the sanity. Is it that prudence creeps cautiously in: the need to earn, do, be what friends and relatives suggest, or just that the body, the soul and the mind cannot for long stand such overheating, and such soldering together, such unifying, and must split again into their familiar component parts, and be manageable?

I took LSD once. I had a vision of the universe and I was part of it, for good or bad and mostly bad, but I tell you it was nothing like being in love. Morality was nothing to worry about: I *was* morality.

I didn't take the pill, Dr Gregory. Nor did I have a coil. I did own a diaphragm, but I had left it behind in Edinburgh, on the dirty bathroom shelf of a rather bad hotel. I never liked it, anyway. I don't suppose it occurred to Joe and Pete that I was, as they say, unprotected. Girls like me – that is to say, bad girls – in their book, knew a thing or two.

Well, either I was not as bad as they thought or I preferred to forget what I knew – the latter is nearer the truth. I wanted Dandy's child, with a great passionate want. I wanted here in the world, in flesh and blood, the growing, thinking, knowing evidence and proof of that love. I wanted the physical manifestation of a spiritual truth. For that is what a child should be, and seldom is, the product of man and woman, of opposing natures, unified, however temporarily, by the amazing, circling, weaving dance of love and lust and God's involvement in it. It is not just the splitting off of a broody woman, who wants something to occupy an empty space in a room and a purpose for her existence, into something as like herself as possible, controllable and guidable and meek – but something new and fierce and different, able to push the whole world a little further on.

111

I loved Dandy, in other words, and I wanted his child.

I was prepared to surrender everything, all I had, for the sake of love. All I had, of course, was my past and my future. I had no property, and no particular position in the world. I expected, I assumed, that Dandy would do the same. That in the intertwining of our limbs was such magic as to make him too surrender everything.

I daresay Jesus felt the same: saying to His disciples, leave all you have and follow me. And they did: left a few fishing nets and a wife or two, no doubt. Peter certainly followed: and upon that rock is built His Church, with all its wealth and worldly power, its gold plate, fornication and corruption, its fat priests and lean inquisitors. The greater the hope, the nearer we aspire to exultation, the more dismal and the deeper the fall.

Perhaps I make too many claims for Dandy and myself? Perhaps the mothers of my girlfriends were right. "Once a man has had you," they'd say, "once he's got what he wants, he no longer respects you. Don't think he'll marry you: he won't."

That was the old wisdom, when girls stayed virgins 'til they married, and did not waste their lives in impractical sexual hankerings, and admired men, and wanted their babies as proofs of love — and indeed, when men gave women babies, and did not just have their sperm snatched from out of them. Then indeed men did despise the girls who slept with them, who could not control their lust. Perhaps Dandy still belonged to the old world: believed the old wisdom. Girls like me you slept with, shacked up with for a bit, but you certainly did not marry them, let alone share your head with them. And when lust faded – men's lust does seem more prone to fade than women's – why, that was the time to move on, and take some decent, flirty, silly virgin out to dinner. She need only, of course, be a spiritual virgin: only a madman, these days, would insist on an actual one.

If that is so, Dr Gregory, then I hate Dandy Ivel, on behalf of a million million hurt and rejected girls.

He did not take me to see his family, I did not meet his friends, he did not take me out in public – only sometimes, with Pete and Joe whispering and furious at the next table – to eat steak and asparagus downstairs in the hotel restaurant. I thought he wanted me all for himself; I thought he wanted to keep the world out, not me in; I thought this was a measure of his love, not his lack of it.

He loved me. I know he did. It *was*, at first, a measure of his love. Only later, when Pete and Joe and his political friends had been at him, did it turn into a useful and prudent measure, to keep me thus so confined.

Men do like to have women confined. In a million million little suburban houses, women are still confined, by love, loyalty and lace curtains. It is not so terrible a fate. All fates are terrible.

In the bedroom Dandy and I still moiled and sweated and groaned, climbing up our mountain of love, whose highest peak, we knew, shone in the reflected glory of God. In the next room Pete and Joe read the financial pages and the

113

political gossip and played cards and smoked cigarettes, and vied with each other in endurance games – they loved to see who could hold a finger longest in the flame of a cigarette lighter – and drank mineral water. Their eyes were bloodshot with smoke. Their fingers were scarred. They were the toads in my Garden of Eden, where I thought I could live for ever.

I did not know they meant to make Dandy Ivel President. I do not think Dandy knew it either. I think it was when he and I were having our affair that they told him. I think that was why he so suddenly changed. Have all this, they said: look down from the mountain of Gethsemane and rule all the world; all you can perceive of earth and sky. But of course you can't have *her* as well. And so love failed, because their timing was so good. The new and major animation quite drowned out and swept away the lesser pain of loss. A week earlier, before the sexual obsession had begun to weaken: a week later, by which time we would have felt ordinary and decent enough to face the world together – and I believe that Dandy would have chosen me, and not America.

I know that since time began men have chosen war, and left women, homes and families. But even so, I believe I nearly won: that Dandy all but thought the world well lost for sake of me. Time, and fate, and chance; accident and conspiracy; all had to contrive to undo us. But so they did.

Dandy no longer knelt before me and worshipped. He knelt before me and was roused, and wished to possess, but also wished to discard, in order to demonstrate that the

114

possession was a trivial matter, not worth having, and that his emotional investment in me had run its course.

He looked through me and beyond me to lands of real power; he no longer saw the boundaries of his kingdom within me. The world was a greater place than he had realised. I sat upon the throne, but I was not a real queen: I was not born to it. No, I was a usurper. I had used women's tricks to enthral him: now the time for my punishment had begun. A different queen must sit upon the throne.

"I love you," he said, "I worship you," but the words ran thin. He did neither. Instead he turned and twisted me upon the bed, and dug his teeth in here and his fingers tweaked there, until I cried out in a mixture of pain and pleasure, and he could use this as evidence against me.

"Kinky cookie," he observed, and though the words were derisive they struck to my heart. He separated himself out from me: his sexual response and mine were different matters. We were no longer equal. He was to be President: I had only existed by courtesy of his fantasy: the pretty, quirky, long-legged, talkative girl he could silence so well and powerfully: now the fantasy faded. I was not the fountainhead of love: I was one of a hundred available girls. Goblets of flesh to be parted and speared and vanquished.

He knelt before me and despised me, and despised himself because in spite of himself his hand would reach out to caress, as if the body had a loyalty, a kindness, and a memory the mind had not. But he wanted now to be all mind, all power, all force and drive; when it came to the choice, he saw women as the warrior's reward, and not their source of strength. Soldiers have a certain way of raping: they pull a woman's skirts over her head and tie them there: now she is faceless, mindless, all body and no identity: no one's wife, no one's sister, no one's mother or daughter, and certainly not herself. That much, even in peace, would be a lot to ask for! She is anyone and everyone's, and if there is a queue for her, so much the better.

"I love you," said Dandy, his mind on the Presidency. "I adore you!" and I felt like such a woman: faceless and sightless, knowing my husband, my brother, my son would be in another queue, in another place: that man is as polite and kind to woman as he can afford to be, and not one whit the more.

And though Dandy fell out of love with me, I did not fall out of love with him. Nothing valuable, I tell myself, is gained for nothing. There is always a price to pay, and I paid it.

Dandy doesn't look at all well, Dr Gregory. When I see his face on television, and I look into his eyes, I see sickness and sadness.

No, of course you can't look into the eyes of someone you see on television. The cameras take a distorted picture to begin with, which is turned into invisible waves, dissolved altogether, before being caught as it flies and crudely re-represented – like a bad cheque at a rude bank – as the original image. What I see can only be a vague representation of the man himself, but I see enough.

Yes, I daresay I see what I want to see. Part of me wants him to die, to crumple up and finish, like a dried up daddy-longlegs in a dusty corner. I want him to be over before I am.'

15

'Only little by little did I realise that the closed world Dandy and I had created for our love had its echo in physical reality. I was, in effect, a prisoner, and as Dandy's enthusiasm faded, so I began to be frightened.

Traffic moved on the street far below. The dome of the Capitol gleamed its mockery of Ancient Rome: great golden eagles perched on copper roosts and squawked derision. In front of the White House the Stars and Stripes hung in brilliant folds. The Potomac glittered and foamed out of the city, away to the East and distant seas, and a home inconceivably far away.

I had become timid, too. So bold in bed, perhaps, that I quite used up all my courage. There was no need for me to leave the hotel: I knew no one in Washington. I had filed my report on Concorde, and the *Star* had printed so edited and rewritten a version of it, and without a by-line, that when Dandy showed it to me I did not at first realise it was mine.

I had telephoned Corin the features editor and said he would not hear from me for some time: that I was off to the South to cover a Ku-Klux-Klan revival. That was while the outside telephone was still working: after I had been living there a week something went wrong with it. It could take incoming calls only. From time to time workmen arrived to fix the instrument, but only seemed to make matters worse.

Since I had no one to telephone this inefficiency made no difference to me. Dandy's office could still contact him, as they increasingly did; and, increasingly, he would respond to their needs and stay away an hour or so, an evening; even, presently, a night. The Senate itself, I discovered, was in recess. This was Dandy's summer holiday. And I could use the internal phone for room service, the beauty parlour, the pool. I had no money, but could run up bills at the boutiques and bookstalls in the lobby.

My own clothes had been washed by the hotel laundry and turned into rags. So now I wore, perforce, what I could buy downstairs. Real silk dresses and cashmere wraps: delicate shoes and rather a lot of jewellery, mostly gold. The beauty parlour had streaked and cut and curled my hair, dyed my eyelashes, waxed my legs.

Dandy liked me to look, as he put it, well-groomed. The difference between the dressed and the undressed, the unspoiled and the spoiled, the cool perfection of the woman dressed and the sweaty imperfection of her undressed and orgasmic was what he loved, and which indeed I much appreciated too. There was, after all, nothing else for me to do but dress and be undressed, wash, and be unwashed again. Why not?

119

There is a certain kind of man who likes women in a mess: as near bed as possible, looking as if their absence from it was accidental and temporary. That they have not had time to comb their hair or wipe the soup stains from a flung-on dress, but must be back in bed again immediately. That has always been rather my style, Dr Gregory, I must admit.

But I have also noticed that men turn us into the women they think they want, and then don't want us any more. Dandy fell in love with an energetic and ambitious young woman with dirty fingernails and within six weeks, by simply doing what she thought he wanted, and what he said he wanted, she had turned herself into a perfumed odalisque, and he didn't want her any more.

Or was it something I did wrong? I hear people say that again and again, sitting tearful among the ruin of love affairs, families, careers. What did I do? Where did I go wrong? Did I say something? As if a single word, a single act, a single flaw, could bring about destruction and desolation. As if we all believed that only by pretending to be something we are not, someone else, biting back the truth, happiness could be achieved. No wonder we all tiptoe through life. Where did I go wrong! I said something wrong! Now I long for Yesterday-ay!

Of course, I have a deformed face. A horse kicked me when I was a child. Hadn't you noticed? My mother's favourite horse. She has his head stuffed and on the wall in the house where I grew up. This is not *my* mouth, *my* chin, *my* nose.

Pete and Joe spent quite a lot of time talking about death, mutilation, rape and destruction. I would overhear them.

They rather unwillingly took me on a sight-seeing tour of Washington, on Dandy's instructions, but spent so much time looking before and behind for rapers and muggers I didn't enjoy it at all. These paranoic fears are catching. The streets thereafter seemed dangerous: full of dark corners where men could, and would, given the half chance – which is all they need – pounce, pin and rape.

I, who had never been afraid of anything or anyone, now saw fearlessness as mere lack of imagination.

As Dandy's love drained away so did my self-esteem. I began to be tearful; to beg and to plead.

Stay with me, don't go, don't you love me any more? What have I done? Do I deserve this? How can you be so cruel?

I would rather not remember that part of it. Joe and Pete crept nearer: I would see the smoke from their cigarettes ooze under my bedroom door before being sucked upward and dissolved by the air conditioning.

One night as I lay tearful, sleepless and alone, the door opened and they came in. Joe sat on the left-hand side of the bed, Pete on the right. They had talked too much about rape for it not to be the first thing I thought of.

Dandy has withdrawn his protection, I thought. He has abandoned me to the servants, the dogs. I am the crumbs from his table; they will snuffle round and lick me up. He has been eating his grand meals in front of their hungry noses for too long. They are greedy, and angry, and hungry.

121

They did not have to say much. Joe sat on the left, Pete sat on the right. The bedclothes effectively pinned me down. My nose ran a little, because I had been crying, and I couldn't move my arms to wipe it.

They sat, they stared. Then Pete moved over.

"You'd better sit up," he said.

The nightie I wore was silk and lace. It had been bought from the boutique down below. This was an hotel where suited executives and politicians came and went, and met their mistresses, and took home such nightdresses as presents to their wives, hoping somehow no doubt to bridge fantasy and reality. Real silk, real lace. Quality!

I had swum naked in mixed company at home and thought nothing of it. A body is a body, I had thought – we had thought, all we girls, in defiance of our mothers – not a means of seduction. A breast will suckle a baby or give and take erotic pleasure if the circumstances are right; otherwise it is of no significance. Bare it or cover it – what does it matter? That the circumstances might be imposed and not chosen had not occurred to me.

"Sit up," repeated Pete. "We have something to show you."

I sat up, and the lace edging of the nightdress fell just below the level of the nipples. I could feel it, but would not look down. Joe stretched out a hand and touched my right breast. "No," said Pete. And Joe pulled the top of the nightdress up for me, smiling, in a friendly and understanding and paternal way, first the right side, then the left until, in their eyes, I was decent again.

"That's more like it," said Joe. And I felt what they wanted me to feel – that I was helpless; that they could rape me if they wanted to, but they didn't, because I was too much like trash even for them: I might infect them with lack of will or self-indulgence or whatever qualities foamed and brewed in the warm hothouse of my body. I existed in the female flesh; I was a receptacle for man's sexual rubbish. And since that, in their reckoning, was what I had chosen, that was all I was.

Americans do not go much for forces beyond anyone's control. So far as they can see, the individual chooses his destiny and his way of life. They have no time for the helpless, the hopeless, the depressed. Those paths, too, seem to have been elected. There is little pity in the rational soul. Certainly Joe and Pete did not pity me.

Pete wanted to show me a photograph in the evening paper. It was of Dandy dining in a restaurant with a young woman. He looked into her eyes and smiled; they raised their glasses and smiled. Those all around smiled too. Dandy's friends and colleagues – the ones I could not meet.

"Youngest Senator toasts Eldest Daughter", said the headline. No doubt she wore a cotton nightie and slept with the window open.

They left the paper with me to read. They went away, but not before Joe's jacket had fallen open, and I had seen the gun strapped beneath his arm.

I read the text. She was the eldest daughter of a banking family, and heir to her grandfather's oil millions. She was one of America's most eligible young women, as Dandy, I was now to understand, was one of America's most eligible bachelors. The adjectives used for Dandy were "shy", "promising", "winning", "brilliant". Hers were "bubbling" and "breathtaking" and "sporty". Wedding bells might yet be heard.

Later, when I worked for the BBC, I tried to trace the cutting back to its source, but never managed to find it. I think perhaps it never existed; except as a figment of the imagination of one of the security agencies to which Pete and Joe were affiliated.

They wanted to be sure I knew my place: to know that I was hopelessly outclassed. Nor was Joe's finger on my breast accidental, but calculated both to frighten and humiliate. It was as if they even knew what nightdress I would wear. Perhaps indeed the bedroom was full of hidden cameras and microphones from the beginning, with or without Dandy's knowledge.

Joe and Pete, I am sure, would be prepared to exchange details of any extramarital sexual experiences with each other, and would see nothing strange in doing so. In a world in which women in bed divide so sharply into two – wives and whores – why not? And perhaps, after all, Dandy was the same. And perhaps the love he professed was nothing but a mockery; the intimacy pretended; the act performed for an audience, and my trust and love merely part of the general entertainment.

Be that as it may, I was by now truly frightened. No one knew where I was. Pete and Joe were armed. Dandy had had enough of me: I could disappear easily enough and no one would know or care or ask questions. That is the drawback of walking proud and free through life without property, debts or credit cards. No mortgage company, no child, no lover of long standing would start enquiring after me. If you care nothing for anyone, nobody cares anything for you. I even wished I wrote more regularly to my mother. Six months without a letter would not worry her at all; and her description of her missing daughter, last heard of in Alabama, would be nothing like that of the girl who shacked up for a time in a Washington hotel, and who then, as such streaked and glossy girls do, moved on.

That night Dandy returned as usual, and I said nothing about the photograph in the paper and pretended to believe the excuses he gave for his absence. I felt a kind of desperate cunning. I marvelled at how I could smile and caress as if everything was normal, and he believed. Deceit is exhilarating: successful deception brings with it a feeling of power. Temporarily, at any rate, these emotions were adequate to sustain me. Presently the shock of lost love would overwhelm them, and the humiliation of false hope: in the meantime I knew I was in danger, and must survive.

Our lovemaking that night was prodigious, and marathon: I knew how to draw it out, and on, by controlling my own responses, organising his. I feigned orgasm, and need, and gratification, pleasure and trust. It was easy enough: I swayed us through love and into lust and back again. In the meantime he was exhausted and I was not, and he slept and I did not, which was what I intended.

His wallet had fallen out of his coat pocket. It was made of soft calf, and stuffed with new dollar bills, which sit finely and flatly together – better than pound notes, which always tend to be used, crumpled and bulky. I left five dollars – in case Dandy needed a taxi in the morning, I suppose – and took the rest. I put on the most boring of my clothes, and the shoes best suited to putting up with feet and walking. I left all the jewellery. Perhaps the eldest daughter could do with it. I looked for my passport where I believed I had left it – in the top drawer of the dressing table. It was not there. All is lost, I thought, and I am as good as dead. But then I found it in the drawer of the bedside table, and opened it, and saw my own imperfect face staring back at me, and felt real and myself again, and braver. I had existed once without Dandy – I could exist without him again.

Joe and Pete, as was their habit, slept on facing sofas in the corridor.

The cold air outside the hotel shocked me. I was not used to it. It seemed to be full of strange smells. It was windy. I could not at first understand what this forgotten feeling was, against my cheek. A buffeting, by something not man-made. I took a taxi to Dulles Airport. I meant to fly to the furthest point the money from Dandy's wallet would allow.

As luck would have it, the money was just enough to take me to London, Heathrow. There was a flight leaving within the hour. And again, as luck would have it, the man I sat next to on the plane, as the adrenalin drained out of my system, shock abated, and the bruising of mind and body and soul began to make itself felt, was Homer.'

16

Before I lost my sight I would sometimes sit and stare for sheer pleasure at the clothes circulating on the other side of the window of the washing machine. Look, there it goes! Laurence's red-spotted shirt, wonderfully wound up with the familiar, paler garments. And there go my white lace pants! How did they get in? Surely the wash is too hot, the spotted shirt contagious with scarlet dye? I would find drama in the washing machine, joy where others found none, in the sheer liberation from domestic drudgery: from rubbing and scrubbing and lifting and wringing.

These days, although I use the dishwasher and the washing machine, I have to trust them to a degree the sighted never do. I have to remember how many programmes ago I put Rinse Aid in the dishwasher: assume the washing machine isn't overflowing, and that all our clothes aren't purple, from the flowing of red and blue dyes.

I have to do something. Let me at least be useful. Laurence offers to do all these things for me, but I do not want him to. I stick by a division of labour that never in the past suited me, but now does. Feminism is a luxury. The world is graded into fit and unfit, not male and female.

Isabel told me she'd been seeing Dr Gregory, one Tuesday morning as I was taking clothes out of the washing machine and putting them in the dryer that stood next to it. She offered to do the task for me, but I preferred that she did not. I like to run my hands over the clothes while they're wet, the better to know them. In the same way hairdressers prefer to cut wet hair rather than dry.

'I'm telling him everything,' she said. 'Do you think that's wise?'
'I imagine that's what you're supposed to do,' I reply.
'I have got so much into the habit of self-deception,' she replied, 'that it comes as rather a shock. If I admit various things to him, I shall presently have to admit them to Homer. I can see it coming.'
'What kind of things?' I ask.
'Fairly fundamental things,' she replied, cautiously.

And she told me about her meeting and marriage with Homer. She met him, she said, by accident.
'Everyone meets their spouses by accident,' I remark.
There is a button missing from the cuff of Laurence's denim shirt. Well, that's all right. The blind can sew on buttons.

She met Homer on an aeroplane. It seemed to be her fate to meet men in the air. Well, it hadn't quite been an accident. He'd been booked for a later flight, but had seen her checking in, wild and beautiful in her apprehension, and had changed his flight to hers, in order to travel with her. It was only years later that he had admitted this. He was not, as he said, in the habit of picking up girls on impulse. But there he was, beside her, as if by accident, and she found him, in her phrase, remarkably easy to talk to.

128

Most men, she claimed, were not: the conversation would be one-sided – about him, not her, and her place in it to utter either prompt or feed lines, smile and look interested, or impressed, or both. True, she admitted, to a stay-at-home what was said by a worldly man was often both interesting and impressive, but the more one got out and about, the less interesting and impressive it became. And she, Isabel, was now well and truly out into the world.

Homer, however, was a man apart. He assumed an easy, confident intimacy which she reciprocated. He wanted to know what she felt, what she thought, where she'd been, where she was going. He was half in love with her at once, both anxious and agreeably possessive and concerned, and she trusted him. Loving Dandy had been a different matter altogether: obsessive and compulsive. This, by comparison, was ordinary, civilised and, in the circumstances, wonderfully comforting.

She did not tell him where she had been, or the manner of her flight or the intensity of her fear.

Most women, running from the love of man, or the shelter of a marital roof, are frightened enough. They fear even the most peaceable and mild of lovers and husbands, as if by rejecting them they will make them monsters. Runaway wives fear punishment, blows; slit throats at worst, broken bones and loose teeth at best. To run from Dandy created terror enough in Isabel's heart; add the fact of Pete and Joe to that, and she was awash with terror and prudence mixed.

She told Homer she'd been covering a story down in Alabama: the country bus she'd been travelling in had caught fire. She'd narrowly escaped with her life, lost all her luggage in the incineration, witnessed horrible scenes, had managed to pick up a few things at a hotel, and, shattered and battered, was now returning home – or if not home, for she had none – back to the comparative sanity, ordinariness and kindness of England.

Whither indeed Homer, for various reasons of his own, to do with the gentleness of society, and man's literary and linguistic heritage, was also fleeing.

Homer offered her a room in the apartment he was renting in Hampstead, until she could get back on her feet.

Proximity, affection, common sense and mutual trust led them presently to the sharing of the room.
'Presently?' I remark. 'How long was presently?'
'A day,' said Isabel. 'I would be much more cautious now, having more to lose. I went to the Clinic almost immediately, and was fitted with a diaphragm.'

It was, I thought at first, an odd detail for her to mention. 'I could see that this was going to be a long-term kind of thing,' she explained, inadequately. 'That Homer was a friend as well as a lover. He would be mine for life, as I would be his, whatever degree of intimacy we decided upon. There was so much comfort in this, you've no idea.'
'Husband, lover, friend, father, all rolled into one,' I say.
'Quite,' she replied.

No wonder, up and down Wincaster Row, we all envied her.

17

'She's cracking,' said Joe, studying the latest print-outs. 'I told you so.'

'It wasn't inevitable,' said Pete.

'You can never trust a whore,' said Joe. 'And one who gives out for nothing is the worst kind of all.'

'She wasn't a whore,' said Pete, 'she didn't take money.'

'She sure as hell did,' said Joe. 'She took the entirety of Dandy's wallet.'

'Only because we left it under her nose,' said Pete.

'She was a whore,' said Joe. 'She took advantage of him the way whores do. She was out for what she could get.'

Both men had been drinking Veuve Clicquot on the rocks to celebrate Dandy's victory in the Primaries. He was now the one, the true, the proper Democratic Candidate. The party had been going on for days. Joe and Pete had kept sober until now. While others cheered, sang, waved banners, threw streamers and marched their hero shoulder high through the streets, Joe and Pete stuck to their guns, their duty, their mineral water. Pippa Dee stayed sober too, and went early to bed each night, since she had a major tournament coming up.

Now the tumult and the joy had died down, and Joe and Pete allowed themselves a little relaxation. They had their feet up on their desks. Joe's wife had girlfriends round; Pete's wife signed up for another evening class.

Presently Pete and Joe thought they ought to check out the girl with the dirty toenails. They drove downtown and followed her out of the nightclub where she worked – the Lousy Buck – to the place where she lived. This turned out to be, as they suspected and feared, an international settlement of Teepee People, white middle-class folk from Europe who lived, in imitation of the Indians, in heavy nylon wigwams and who for their annual outing shipped over to the banks of the Potomac river. Their children ran wild, grimy, badly nourished and covered with sores.

'Holy Mary,' said Joe, as his polished shoes encountered mud and pebbles. 'Now I understand why her feet are so filthy.'

Yellow mud squelched up between Vera's toes. She changed out of her earning clothes into the embroidered robes, heavy with grease and dirt, favoured by the Teepee People. She smoothed her hair with oil and bound it back tightly with a cord. She was alone in the tent; her eyes smarted with wood smoke.

'Keep well clear of that wood-fire smoke,' whispered Pete to Joe, 'it's carcinogenic. More hazardous to the lungs even than tobacco.'

They watched Vera from a slit in the tent canvas. The river rustled behind them. The lights of Washington made the sky yellowy, so that the stars were pale. The Teepee People, unpolluted by employment, gathered round a wood fire and chanted mournful tunes and ate barbecued chicken legs. The children and the dogs got what they could snatch of the gnawed bones. That was traditional.

Pete and Joe, whose own children ate balanced meals and had vitamin supplements, were distressed to see it.

Vera calmed herself with a drag or two of marihuana, and munched a couple of pills, and wandered off to join her companions. She was squaw to Smoky Al, who was seventy-two but virile. She shared this position with her sister Marielle. They were Dutch girls in flight from repressive bourgeois parents. Vera was twenty-four and Marielle twenty-two.

Pete and Joe snatched Vera in the shadows between teepee and fire, and dragged her off into their car. Surprise and strength made resistance or noise impossible. No one noticed her abduction.

'We don't intend to hurt you,' said Joe, lying. 'We just need to ask you a few questions.'
'Holy Mary, how she stinks,' said Pete, stepping on the accelerator.
'It's musk,' she explained, as if one insult or another, in whatever circumstance, made little enough difference to her. 'I'd wash more but there's no running water. Besides, there's nothing to be ashamed of in body smells.'

Pete and Joe were unconvinced. They took her to an apartment they knew about from old times, where no questions were asked, except by them, and where for the sake of old friendships they were still welcomed, and there, under bright lights, interrogated her.

They satisfied themselves she was in no one's pay; neither Gaddafi's, the KGB's nor that of any United States security agency's, but had bedded with Dandy because he asked her.

'Are you in the habit of doing it because you're asked?'

'Yes,' she replied.

They'd punched her and humiliated her, stripped her and mocked her, but had stopped short of sexually assaulting her. She thought they were crazy; driven that way by their life style. Pete reminded her of her father. She was not particularly afraid. She had tripped so many times on so many substances she was as likely to freak out at a harmless puff of smoke as at anything else. She was more frightened by her own thought processes than by guns, threats and blows. Why they behaved as they did, not what they did, was what got her. Smoky Al got his kicks out of punching and pinching, anyway.

'Listen you guys,' she said. 'I'll tell you everything you want, just give me time to speak.'

They stopped threatening, and listened.

She told them she'd taken Dandy back to the teepee. She fancied him. She didn't want his money, only his body. Or rather Smoky Al did, via her. Smoky Al liked her to go with younger men in the evenings. He thought it kept him virile. That way, in fact, lay immortality. She could always pick up some young man at the Lousy Buck, glimmering at him from the back of the Hat Check room.

'Holy Mary Mother of God!' said Joe, appalled at the use Dandy's manhood had been put to.

But the episode, she told them, had not ended as she had expected. Dandy, for all his energy and good looks had not – to put it crudely – been able to get it up. She'd done her best, but he had ended weeping and crying all over her, and talking about some red-headed Australian girl he'd loved and lost.

'Lots of guys are like that these days,' she complained. 'Sexual inadequates. At least Smoky Al's reliable.'

Joe and Pete went into the bathroom to discuss what to do next. It was a grimy place. No one had washed out the bath for months. Someone had spat blood into the basin. Security demanded that women did not come here – at least not of their own accord – and since the men who came were the kind who felt that cleaning was women's work, and demeaning, little was done. The tap, which Joe turned on to cover the sound of their conversation ran red with rust.

Their conversation was brief.

'You or me?' asked Joe.
'You,' said Pete, kindly.
'Sure,' said Joe, 'and it's a terrible thing for a man to have a training, and no use to put it to. So the time has come at last.'

Joe shot her, and his jacket swung back nicely because of the weights his wife had sewn in the lining, and didn't

135

interfere with his arm, and she died cleanly and swiftly, as they put it, snuffing out for real as she had done so many times in practice, sniffing this or munching that. The weapon, also a gift from his wife, behaved as efficiently and well as he knew it would.

As Pete remarked – for Joe, after the deed, seemed fidgety and uneasy, and not suffused by postcoital calm, as he had vaguely supposed he would – they could hardly have let Vera go round Washington claiming the Democratic Candidate to the Presidency to be a sexual inadequate. If she'd chosen her words more carefully, shown sense or self control or a due reverence for anything at all, she could perhaps have lived. They could have frightened her, impressed her, even changed her memory of the event, if the money and the will and the time were available; stopped her mouth, in fact, by any number of means. But it seemed easier, and kinder, and more honourable, simply to stop her; to put her out of the misery of a wretched and degraded life. She would never make it back up the steep, boring, hygienic path to wife and motherhood, freedom and happiness. The dirt was ground in between her toes: there for life.

An ambulance came in response to a phonecall or so to former colleagues, and the body was taken away. No one would miss her. Wandering girls without wedding rings or property, cast out by their families, whose friends are too vague or too high to ask questions, disappear every day, for lesser reasons.

Joe said a Hail Mary or so on the way back to the office. He had stopped fidgeting but complained that he felt no different for having taken a human life.

'It was a very negligible kinda life,' said Pete.
'Perhaps that's why.'

Next time they saw Dandy, they agreed, they would put it to him that picking up girls had to stop now, once and for all. It did him no good, and them no good – though quite how much no good they would of course not mention. 'Lessons from Watergate one, two and three,' said Pete. 'Leave the people up there out of it.'

They had used McSwain's name on the telephone, when organising the ambulance. He would know enough of what had happened by now not to want to know more. That some new riverbank Jezebel had had her hands eaten by dogs –

Now they punched up Isabel Rust's coding on the computer, and were not happy with what they saw. For Isabel had done what they had assumed could not be done – she had climbed the slippery path out of the mire of self-disgust and degradation, on to the high clean slopes of respectability. She associated, moreover, with the influential and the famous.
'We must have misjudged this dame,' said Pete, cautiously. 'She might have class.'
We're in a very highly sensitive area here,' agreed Joe. 'No two ways about it.'

They worked out an assortment of scenarios for the future. There was one in which Dandy broke off his engagement to Pippa Dee, Homer divorced Isabel as a result of a liaison with Sandy Elphick, Jason was claimed by the President as his child, Dandy and Isabel married, and Isabel Rust ended up in the White House, as First Lady, to the consequent betterment of trade links with Australia. That one made them laugh a lot. The only snag being that *she'd* have to be the first lady President, because *he* sure as hell wouldn't be the next male one.

Both, by midnight, were feeling invigorated and cheerful. The gun in Joe's shoulder-holster had a warm and powerful tang to it which it had never had before. He was too sheepish about it to mention it to Pete, but offered up a silent prayer of thanks to holy Mother Mary, lily pure.

Pete put their one photograph of Isabel, Homer and Jason on the top of the filing cabinet. It was safe enough there from Dandy's eyes. On his rare visits to the Evans building he went straight by VIP lift to the Penthouse, bypassing lowlier floors.

'That boy needs a haircut,' observed Pete of Jason.

'Sweet Jesus,' said Joe, 'if that boy had a haircut, we wouldn't be talking we'd be acting. And fast.'

He masked out Jason's hair with a piece of card, and the likeness to Dandy was startling.

'Even so,' said Pete. 'I don't like to see her making a sissy out of him.'

'The gays run San Francisco,' said Joe.

'This is Washington,' said Pete, 'and I thank God for it.'

They mentioned the Holy Family quite a lot, one way and another: there is, after all, a human need to seek higher authority, and earthly ones had proved fallible once or twice too often.

'Lessons from Watergate four, five and six. Put your trust in God, not in Man,' as Joe observed.

Pete worried a little to Joe about the possibility that Vera, too, like Isabel, might have made it out of the slime, had she been left alone. Joe thought no: she hadn't the brain. And Isabel, it had been obvious at the time, had been one hell of a smart cookie. Vera had been just too far gone, as a piece of fabric sometimes wears too thin for mending. They had done the right thing – by Vera, by themselves, their candidate, God, Jesus, Mary and America.

The next day Pippa Dee thoroughly trounced her opponent – 6-2, 6-2, game, set and match. She won fairly, or as fairly as a match can be won, when one of the players seems set fair to be First Lady in the White House and wears a tennis dress by Dior; and the other is an ex-cheerleader from Oregon, dressed ordinarily if sensibly by Adidas, and the crowd applauds whenever she misses a point.

18

'I don't know why other people have babies,' said Isabel to Dr Gregory the following week, 'but I know why I had one. It was in an attempt to weigh myself down, to stop myself drifting, to give myself a sense of purpose, a point of obligation. Or put it another way. I felt I was polishing away at the thinly silvered surface of my life with the most abrasive of steel wools; unfocused emotion, and grief, and sex, a racing pulse and a racing mind, all wound raggedly and jaggedly together, and I had worn through to tin, and rust, and a rub or so more and I'd be through to the hollow, the black nothingness within. I had to fill myself up from the centre out. I knew it. I had to become solid; little by little replace what I had worn away. You know how they pack a wound in hospital? Feed in fold after fold of gauze, so a scab can't form, but the flesh must heal from the bottom up? Each day the gauze is removed, and fresh fed in, a little less each day, until eventually the wound is no more; and the scab is allowed to form. It is a very lengthy and very painful process. Proper healing, I suppose, usually is. Nothing is for nothing.'

Dr Gregory had fitted Isabel in with no trouble at five o'clock on two consecutive evenings. It had made some complications in her rota with Homer, but they had sorted it out. Jason's haircut had had to be put off. Both Homer and Isabel liked his hair the length it was but Mrs Pelotti had said, 'I don't suppose you care whether Jason is a boy or a girl, but he'd like to be one or the other, I daresay. Do him a favour. Get him a haircut.'

But Mrs Pelotti, both agreed, could not totally rule their lives. And as Jason insisted that Isabel, not Homer, took him to the hairdresser, his hair would just have to stay long for a time longer, while Isabel talked to Dr Gregory – about herself, and Homer, and Jason.

'To forgo a child for a career seems to me ridiculous. To seek fulfilment through a child equally ridiculous. The career can provide a kind of sickly status, and leisure can be a pleasurable experience, but happiness is not usually found by those who seek to organise it. And the child, once born, is its own being, and is all work, and as likely to reflect disgrace as credit on its parents. The more you seek to make the child in your own image, the more elusive he or she becomes.

'I have a neighbour, Hilary. She is a feminist and she has a little daughter, only three, who will creep into my bedroom and use my cosmetics, if we take our eyes off her for a moment: She sidles up to men and rubs against their legs, as a female kitten might. Nothing is what one expects.'

'We are talking about you,' said Dr Gregory, 'not the neighbours.'

141

'Quite so,' said Isabel. 'Let me go into a little clinical detail. When I met Homer on the plane my period was a week late. That may have been because I was pregnant, or merely because my menstrual cycle was upset. Emotion can do that for you, of course. I made love with Homer a couple of days after I met him. Four weeks later my period had still not started and I concluded, and a doctor confirmed, that I was indeed pregnant.

Now, Dr Gregory, the baby could have been Dandy's and might have been Homer's. Most young women of my class and kind, even wanting a baby but finding themselves in such uncertainty, would have had the pregnancy terminated and started again with one more clearly attributable. I think I would do such a thing now. No, I had no feelings against abortion. A woman in her lifetime chooses, of the twenty or so possible pregnancies she could expect if she lived as a savage, to bring only some two or three babies to term. The method of rejection by which she selects these babies is usually traumatic, and always unnatural, whether it's by clinging to her virginity or by sexual deviancy, contraception or abortion. The latter I knew to be a wretched business, but my life of late had been wretched enough. On my return from America I crept round Homer's apartment as if frightened my foot would indent the carpet too much and I would be blamed. I felt washed up, by high tides of luck and chance: a kind of bleached-out driftwood. I felt like an unsuccessful whore, who has offered herself for hire and found no takers.

And now I was pregnant – good for something, and a kind of perverse excitement reasserted itself in me. Dandy's baby. Oh yes, surely Dandy's baby. Reason told me it could be

Homer's, but I knew the way of the world by now, the patterns made by fate, the brushstrokes of event. Dandy's baby. The part of him that loved me; the part of me that loved him, taken flesh and glorious.

Did you ever steal when you were a child? Do you remember the mixture of excitement, glee, fear, and terrifying triumph as you snatched a handful of sweets from Woolworth's counter? That was what I felt like. Dandy's baby! Stolen, whipped away, under the noses of Pete and Joe. A secret victory, which no one would ever know.

Easy enough to tell Homer the baby was his. Easy enough to more or less believe it myself. Easy enough to feel that the protecting, loving, friendly arm around my shoulder as I retched and moaned was the man I loved, the real, the spiritual father of my child.

But now two things have happened, Dr Gregory. First, Jason himself is uneasy and unhappy. The mother forgets so easily that the baby is not the figment of her imagination, the product of her love and her concern, but his own person, the centre of his own universe, not peripheral to hers. But there it is, and as the baby grows to be a child, too big for the mother to pick up and run with, for more than a yard or two, she must acknowledge it. Jason has rights in this matter, too. And secondly, as the child grows older his parentage becomes more obvious, and soon even Homer will see it, or have it suggested to him.

And thirdly, for there is this to consider too, if I am a public servant, if I am to speak to millions and take their thoughts and feelings this way and that, should I not have some degree of integrity myself? Should I not myself be a servant of the truth?

You look startled, Dr Gregory, but the media, as it's called, is the new priesthood, and beyond Homer, Jason's and my own difficulties lies a greater duty, and a greater obligation.

Well, one step at a time! And that, I see, is what I have been doing.

The first step on the road up this frightening and menacing mountain was the having of the baby. My motives were mixed, of course they were; a confusion of the silly, the serious, the malicious and the marvellous. Nevertheless, the care of a baby, the sheer boring, repetitive, purposeful nature of the task is a great purifying agent. Bad is sifted out, leaving good behind. The second step was the acquiring of a house and a home: even such a thing as the paying of rates is an acknowledgement of the community around and one's duty to it. The third step, yet to be taken, is to tell Homer the truth.'

The room filled with silence. The fig tree rubbed against the pane.
'I see,' said Dr Gregory, eventually. 'That is to be the further punishment of your husband, for what you see as your father's dereliction.'

Isabel laughed.
'You can't win, can you?' she observed.
'No,' he replied, 'inasmuch as it isn't a battle, but a civil war waged within the self, in which there can be no victors.'
'So you are advising me not to tell Homer?'

144

'It would be unprofessional of me to advise you one way or the other. I can only help you understand your motives.'

'Nevertheless, that's what you're advising.'

He said nothing, and she took that as assent.

19

The newspaper is pushed through the letter box every morning between seven and seven-fifteen. The letters come a little later. A squeak of metal as the flap is opened, the dull grate of paper wedging and abrading against the sharp edges of the slit – a thud and a plop, and lo, the outside world is there within, and those that hath eyes to see, let them make of it what they will.

The postman wakes me every weekday morning. That is to say, the quality of my darkness changes.

Bills. Laurence reads them aloud to me, groaning and moaning, but I know he is secretly proud of the vast sums required, and the fact that he can pay them, and that the dreadful, gnawing financial anxiety that dogged our early days is gone. I don't, in retrospect, know what we worried about. We were young, we ate, and slept, and wore shoes, and had a roof over our heads, somehow. And we *saw*, we all *saw*. If the electricity was cut off, we could improvise. If the bailiffs repossessed our treasures, there was time to accumulate more. When we are old, I suppose, the anxiety will return, and with more reason. When you can no longer pay for the roof over your head, someone else does it, in a grudging, parsimonious way. The old, like forsaken females, are expected to put up with second best, as a payment for misfortune.

Isabel told Homer. She told him on a Sunday night. Most domestic murders happen over the weekend. In some cities in the USA, statistics show us, it is safer for a woman, who is anxious about her survival, to be at home during the week and on the street at weekends.

Homer of course did not murder Isabel, but she crept into my house on the Monday morning, early, like a kind of wraith. There was only one letter that morning; Mondays are an easy day for the postman. Offices have been shut over the weekend: no bills have been serviced. New work is initiated at the beginning of the week. Laurence's telephone goes most on Tuesdays and Wednesdays, and hardly at all on Friday afternoons. People are tired.

20

Picture the scene! It is night. The husband sleeps between dainty sheets, the sleep of the just and the righteous. Familiar pictures hang upon the walls: landscapes seen a thousand times. Framed photographs of the child stand upon a mantelpiece: the newborn baby, the beaming toddler, the earnest infant schoolgoer, wide-eyed.

The bedside lamp is on: a gentle glow; the better one would imagine to stir the imagination of the lovemaker than assist the reading of a newspaper on a dark winter morning. In the ashtray is an almost entirely unsmoked cigarette, stubbed out. Homer's campaign is working.

The wife paces. The events of the world crowded forward. The past surged in to overwhelm the present: it is night. Fears and fancies assault even the waking soul, as the nightmare visitor makes his presence felt, roaming the limits of the conscious mind, unable to effect his proper entry into the dreaming self. Supposing they *know*, thinks Isabel. . . . Supposing I am being watched? Surely I must be a danger to them? Supposing they mean to kidnap Jason? Kill me? Her mind will not even contemplate the yet severer fact — that Jason would be better dead — the heir to the throne, by right of precedence but not expediency. Supposing even now they stand outside, under the lampposts of Wincaster Row, watching – in the way I could expect from a hundred films seen, a hundred books read? Perhaps the stuff of thriller fantasy is real: perhaps the whole way of life of the cosily domestic is by permission, not by right? Is granted only while the eyes of the mighty look the other way, with casual, short-lived kindness.

Isabel draws the curtains, looks. No one.

Homer takes a deeper breath. She listens, counts; in every seven breaths of her sleeping husband one is drawn deeper than the others; as one in every seven waves – or so rumour has it amongst the builders of sand castles – is stronger, higher than the rest: the one to wait for, in dread and in exhilaration.

The feeling of menace, of fright increases, and with it a kind of wariness. The emotion is too acute, surely, to have its basis in reality, here in this room where nothing happens. Except the sleeping husband breathes, and the child upstairs, and the mood of the house keeps pace, earlier images of earthquake washed away by the drone of the Hoover, the click of the cat door, the purr of the inefficient refrigerator: the sounds and habits of everyday life. Surely everything can be, will yet be, as it was before?

No. Now listen to the words. The gist of what is said; the grist of contention; the kernel of the hard nut of change.

'Homer,' says Isabel, waking her husband, 'there is something I have to tell you. I need your advice. I am frightened.

This is something we have to face together. Dr Gregory says I shouldn't tell you but he expects a strength from me I haven't got. I have reason to believe that Jason is not your son, but Dandy Ivel's. He who is soon – by all accounts – to be President of the United States of America. Your country –' she added, as if she could modify the shock by attributing at least some of the blame to her husband.

'Isabel,' said Homer, sitting up, 'what fantasy is this? If I will not do in your fevered mind as father for Jason and you must look for a better one, why not pick Prince Charles? At least he's nearer home.' He lay down again and closed his eyes.

'Homer,' said Isabel. 'He looks like Dandy Ivel. He doesn't look like Prince Charles.'

'Ever since you went to see Dr Gregory,' observed Homer, eyes still closed, 'you've been very peculiar.'

'It was your idea I went,' said Isabel, and being now at a normal level of wakefulness, she began to lose her fears, and wish she had never spoken.

'Oh forget it,' she said, 'go back to sleep.'

But Homer did not obligingly fall back into slumber.

He got out of bed as she got into it, and began to dress.

'Where are you going?' she asked.

'I don't see why I should put up with this,' he said. 'I take it as an insult. I don't want to be at the receiving end of your neuroses. If I was the kind of father who ignored his child and left everything to the mother, and you spoke to me in the way you just have, in your thoroughly vicious attempt to deny me, I could perhaps understand and forgive it, but I'm not, and I can't. Jason is as much my child as yours.'

'Homer,' said Isabel, 'I had an affair with Dandy Ivel, just before I met you.'

'You're pathetic,' he repeated. 'Is your own life so shallow and futile that you have to claim some kind of liaison with the great and famous?'

'Homer, where are you going?'

'I'm going away,' he said. 'I can't stay under the same roof as you. I just don't want to. How many other people are you telling the same story to? Do you realise how insulting you are being to me? How damaging to poor little Jason?'

'I haven't told anyone,' she lied.

'I've lived with you long enough to know when you're lying, Isabel,' he said.

'But Homer,' said Isabel, 'I have to work tomorrow and if you're not here how will I manage with Jason?'

'You should have thought of that before,' he said, in thin-lipped victory. 'Why not ask Dandy Ivel?'

Isabel tried to stand between Homer and the door. She could not give up the notion that her husband would at once understand, forgive and render assistance. She had grown careless and sleepy, as a sentry might who has occupied an uneventful post too long; who has heard too many twigs snapping to believe them footsteps any more.

She had been a wife too long, had come to believe that she and Homer were as one: apple branch grafted on to pear branch, perhaps, but now well and truly grown into each other; their interests coinciding.

Not so.

As if to demonstrate their total separateness, Homer hit Isabel. Her restraining hand, laid upon his left arm, some-how gave his right arm permission to swing back and then swing forward, so that his hand caught the side of her face with a hard hand-slap.

Men, in Isabel's world, did not hit women. The Foster's men, back home in the outback, the red-faced, windblown sunburnt men of the outback, who trampled flowers and kicked dogs and cheated her mother – they hit women, and believed that women liked and needed blows, and hit each other a great deal, too, and perhaps thought they were real only when in pain. But Homer?

Homer himself seemed startled. There were, she saw to her surprise, tears in his eyes. He shook his head at her, as if to indicate he was beyond words, and left the room. She nursed her swelling face: pain came back into her jaw, as it had been so many years ago, when her mother's horse had kicked her mouth, and she wept, both from the shock of this event, and the remembered trauma.

She heard him go into the bathroom; then down into the hall to collect his coat, and out the front door. She was left in silence, and desolation.

She went into the bathroom later and found he had taken his toothbrush, and his waxed dental floss, from which she understood that he would be at least a night away.

She assumed he would presently return, in the same way as she assumed no one would try to kill Jason – any notion to the contrary being too terrible to consider.

She looked at herself in the mirror – the perfect, candid eyes and brow; the rather stern nose, the disfigured jaw;

and saw herself as entirely accidental. The mirror was one Homer had picked up in a junk shop. It was in the style of fifty years ago – bright glass with bevelled edges, and a flange of mirror to either side, so that the full face stared back in single innocence, and the profiles were flung back and forth, like a ball, from one reflection to the other, receding into infinity.

'I only wanted to speak the truth,' she said aloud to her simple, single reflection, and even as she spoke knew she lied, and that this could hardly be the whole story. But the side mirrors seemed to catch the essence of what she said, and bounced it to and fro, back into the recesses of infinity, as if, in spite of herself, she had ceased to be an accidental creature, misbegotten and misbegetting, and become purposeful and of significance.

Upstairs, Jason started to cry. Dawn was breaking: a cold light gleamed round the edges of the drawn curtains. She realised she had not slept at all. She went upstairs to Jason; he was half asleep, whimpering.

'It's all right. What's the matter?'
'I dreamt there was a white light and a bang and when I looked everything was just stone, and I couldn't see you, and I looked and looked but you were never there, and I hadn't any hands, just sort of strings.'

'It's all right,' said Isabel, 'it's all right,' but she knew it wasn't. She knew the dream was shared, and came out of past realities and present fears: that the whole world tiptoed round, holding its breath, for fear that with a cough or a sneeze the dream would become real. That the very fabric

153

of the walls, the mobile above the child's bed, the books on the shelves, the people who loved and strived and quarrelled in their search for perfection, would all, all vanish in a twinkling, fading faster even than a dream, and all aspiration be set at nought, mind turned into air, flesh into string.

Jason sat up. The dream had evaporated. His mother, after all, still ran his world. What Isabel said was real.
'It was only a dream,' he said, confident again. 'It wasn't true.'
'It wasn't true,' she repeated.
'Is it time to wake up?' he asked.
'No. Go back to sleep,' she said, and obedient for once he did, sleeping soundly and peacefully, until the proper time for his normal waking shout, five minutes' grace, and then the commencing tumult of his day.

21

'Truth?' Elphick seemed puzzled. Isabel was bleary-eyed, distraught and less coherent than usual. They sat in the viewing room together, in that companionship of shared interests, shared difficulties, which makes comrades of even the most unlikely people. They watched clips of flood water, swarming bees and crawling ants. 'Television is a strange place in which to seek truth, still less declaim it.'

The programme included a scientist who believed the Thames Flood Barrier was more likely to swamp London than save it, and could prove it; a woman who told fortunes by watching the behaviour of ants; and a man who fed dye to his bees and produced coloured honey. There were too many insects on the programme – a glaringly obvious fact which seemed to have altogether eluded Alice the researcher. Elphick's wife had left him, and since this event he had remained sober and faithful to her memory, as he had not been to her in actuality. At any rate these days he failed to take Alice home to his London flat. Their relationship, never properly acknowledged in the first place, was drifting into nothingness, leaving Alice confused, unable to concentrate on her work, and an object of pity to everyone, it seemed, except Elphick. 'If she goes on like this,' he observed to Isabel, 'they'll have to make her a producer. They can't fire her because of her contract; and we can't put up with her; so she'll have to be promoted. That's how people rise to the top of organisations: the scum that gets thrown up as the great yeast seethes and brews.'

He spoke calmly, without animosity. Alice had been relegated, it seemed to Isabel, back into the seething ranks of the enemy: those who thwarted Elphick's intentions and confounded his purposes.

'Do you have a black eye?' he asked, looking at her closely, suddenly personal.

'Yes,' said Isabel.

'Who?' asked Elphick.

'My husband.'

'How interesting,' he said. 'If you go to Make-up they'll patch it up at least a little and you'll spread less alarm and despondency amongst the team. The week's programme is cause for enough, without you adding to it.'

He turned his attention back to the screen. Ants waved their mandibles at him.

'I think you have a small appetite for truth,' he said. 'Most people do. We all deal in agreeable fictions – that we are loved, or cared for, or needed.'

'You just feel bitter,' she said, 'because your wife is gone.'

'And you want to speak the truth on television because your husband has blacked your eye. What sort of truth do you mean, Isabel?'

'I have the ear of millions,' she said. 'All I have to do is turn to them and speak the truth.'

He laughed.

'You have a conspiracy to reveal? The Prime Minister is a

KGB mole? The BBC is run by the Chinese Triad? The country is punch drunk with revelations. You would only lose your job, Isabel, and the respect of the millions. You would be labelled freak and hysteric: an ego-tripper.'

'But you don't know what I want to say, Elphick.'

'Word gets round,' he said, and after that refused to discuss the matter, except to add that if she wanted to put in a plea to animal lovers to fight for the dismantling of the Thames Flood Barrier she could by all means do so. Dogs and cats were badly hit by floods, and hysteria on their behalf one of the few socially acceptable forms of that condition.

A bee rolled its many-faceted eye at Isabel. Microphotography zoomed in to show that the lidless rims of the eyes were gnawed by little white translucent parasites, who waved tiny limbs in energetic glee, and seemed to enjoy their life.

'It's disgusting,' said Elphick. 'Alice is really going to have to go.'

Over lunch in the canteen Dandy Ivel was much discussed. Isabel had the uneasy feeling that people looked at her to see how she would react – and told herself no, she imagined it. She was tired, upset, suffering from lack of sleep and a black eye, and too ready to imagine such things.

Dandridge Ivel, unafraid, had given an interview to *Playboy*. If the truth ruined him, as it had all but ruined Jimmy Carter, too bad, said Dandy. Yes indeed he lusted after women in his heart, and in the flesh too. What the unmarried and the childless did to each other or with each other was no one's business but their own. But marriage remained

157

a sacrament, as was the begetting of children, and the procreation of children and the act of sex could not be separated.

'Good God,' said Elphick, in admiration. 'He'll get the swingers' vote but not lose the Catholics.'

The word black for Isabel's eye now seemed a misnomer. The flesh around the eye had turned from a greyish mottled colour threaded with thin brilliant green lines to a browny-blue puffiness. Make-up had done their best with it. Today was rehearsal day, and Isabel's appearance of no consequence. Two days later, in front of the cameras, the show transmitted live into the houses of millions, it would certainly matter.

'You may not be able to go on,' said Elphick.
'That's ridiculous,' said Isabel. 'Say I walked into a broom handle.'
'Nobody believes stories like that however true they may be. Besides, you're in a funny mood. You might stray from the script or read the autocue wrong and bring us all into disgrace. I'll see how you are on Thursday.'

So resolution faded, thought Isabel, in the face of habit, exhaustion, physical discomfort, the mockery of others and the defining force of words, which reduces the vague and the great to the certain and small.

Later she called Dr Gregory and cancelled her appointment, through his receptionist. She felt she had nothing to say to him: that her present now so overwhelmed her past that she could not for the time being afford the luxury of nostalgic emotion. She called Homer's office, pretending to be Alice, and was told that Homer was in New York, but was expected back at the end of the week.

'Wasn't that rather sudden?' asked Isabel. 'I spoke to him only yesterday and he said nothing about New York.'
'It was rather sudden,' said the girl, shortly, and put the phone down. Isabel felt she had been recognised, and suffered. Her eye deepened its blues and felt stiff, but was oddly comforting, as if Homer were with her, and she was used to that.

Rehearsals went badly. The fortune teller complained that the lights overstimulated the ants and made prediction difficult. The honey maker unexpectedly disclosed a degree of toxicity in the colouring agent in which he soaked his frames. The water engineer had a difficult, falsetto voice. There was union trouble in one of the other studios, and the camera crew were edgy. Two of the cameras failed simultaneously, replacements were unavailable – or at any rate Elphick, by then beside himself with ill temper and spite, claimed they were – and the rehearsal was postponed until the following morning.

Elphick had not brought his car. Alice offered to drive him home.
'Don't bother,' said Elphick. 'Isabel will do it. Won't you, Isabel.'
'Very well,' said Isabel.

But she was chilled by the look of despair on Alice's face. Elphick's wife was gone; there was a void to be filled and Alice was not to be allowed to fill it. Her life lay shattered and meaningless, as the lives of women so often are who hand their feelings and their future into the safekeeping of married men. Chilled though Isabel was, laying claim to sisterhood as she did, still she went out with Elphick, triumphant under Alice's pink and anxious nose, and felt a disturbing degree of pleasure at thus being party to Alice's distress.

Once in the car she trembled and was ashamed of herself, but she had done what she wanted. There was no virtue in remorse. She planned to sleep with Elphick, and he, it was fairly clear, with her; Alice would just have to look after herself.

They drove to his apartment in silence. The scars that criss-crossed his face were pale, the skin around them flushed. She remembered the apple tart her mother used to make on Sunday mornings – pink apple crossed with pale pastry strips: always slightly undercooked.

She laughed, but could hardly explain the joke to Elphick.

The traffic moved slowly. It was the rush hour. She felt free of guilt and childishly happy and, wondering why, remembered that she had asked Jennifer to collect Jason from school, and look after him until her return from work. So accustomed had she become to Homer's help – or rather, his determined, relentless sharing – that she had until now quite forgotten the existence of neighbours and friends, baby-sitters and practical well-wishers – the safety net that mothers of young children weave for themselves, with varying degrees of dexterity. She, Isabel, had simply failed to weave one at all.

'The lights are green,' remarked Elphick. Horns behind her blared. She moved forward to the next intersection.

To live in a house with Homer, it occurred to Isabel, was like living in a house made dark by a massive oak tree, planted four square before the front door. When you opened the door the tree blotted out the light. And now the tree was gone, wrathfully uprooted, and when she opened the door – yes, there was the hideous hole, raw and gaping and painful, and immeasurably deep and untidy, but on the other side of it was a wide, bright landscape, stretching as far as she could see, and when the hole was just a little closed, a little healed, she would be free to wander in it at will, hand in hand with Jason. Jason hers; not theirs. And other people, other women, would wander out of their houses on to the hills, and they would wave to each other, and the children would play and there would be nothing but laughter and peace.

She laughed at this child's version of paradise. Like a child's picture, it was flawed and impossibly naïve.

'Isabel,' said Elphick, 'do concentrate. You're even worse than Alice. Is it something I do to women?'
'I don't think so,' she said, moving on.

Women, as everyone kept saying, were people too, and no doubt stood oak-like in front of men's doors, similarly blotting out light. Nor was child's play a matter of laughter and peace, but of the testing out of the most elaborate and often disagreeable of adult rituals. And the company of women was better, it was true, than the company of men, but usually only if those women had men to go home to.

161

So men, no doubt, had thought about the company of other men. Everything changed, but not much improved.

'Do you always laugh when you drive?' enquired Elphick. 'I seldom do. I usually cry.'

'I'm sorry,' she said, and this time ground the gears as she started off. He raised his eyebrows but said nothing. She observed that his hand, pale, bony and long, lay on her thigh. She had not noticed when he placed it there, but had taken it as a matter of course. The pressure of his forefinger increased in unmistakable sexual invitation.

'I don't love Homer,' said Isabel, surprising even herself. 'I'm glad he's gone. I will be sorry when he returns.'

'When your black eye has vanished,' said Elphick, 'I daresay you'll feel differently. Love is a very difficult thing to define. Perhaps now is not the right time to try.'

'I've been convalescing, that's all,' said Isabel. 'From my childhood, and my youth. And then I had this really bad attack of love –'

'Let's not talk about love,' said Elphick. 'Let's not overload this situation any more than we need. And let us not talk about husbands and wives, or make any excuses for our behaviour. Let us simply accept that we are miserable sinners, and have a good time.'

She found, by some miracle, a parking place directly outside Elphick's door.

His apartment had that uneasy opulence more typical of film than television people – of hard times punctuated by stupendously good times. Worn sofas and a Braque painting; rickety dining chairs and an onyx coffee table. In the bookcases were the paperbacks of his youth, yellowing. *The*

Catcher in the Rye, A Certain Smile, Lucky Jim, Koestler, Eliot and Auden – *The Making of the English Working Class* – and Isabel felt a pang of grief for him, that almost did for real liking.

He saw her reading the titles.

'The literature of one's youth,' he said. 'Sad. So much for aspiration.'

'What did you aspire to?'

'I wanted to save the world, like anyone else. Now I'm producer of a mediocre talk show, with a wife who's left me and children who've grown out of me, and nothing left but the slow decline downhill to redundancy and death.'

In the face of so much gloom, desire failed.

'Perhaps I'd better go,' she said.

'There,' he said. 'I've depressed you. The only person I don't seem to depress is Alice, and that's because she's even gloomier than me. I thought you would make a change, Isabel. So bright and positive, even with a black eye.'

He handed her a mirror, of the kind that Pan traditionally hands the naked Venus; long-handled, gilt-surrounded. She studied her bruised eye, and desire returned.

'Yes, but Elphick,' she said, 'I don't understand myself.'

He watched the expressions on her face change, as the sea changes when the wind blows over it, turning from benign to menacing and back again, during the space of a breath or so.

'Don't let's go into all that,' he said, 'all that psychological stuff,' dismissing doubt, recrimination, motive, purpose and scruple – the very stuff of her life with Homer – with so male and easy a wave of the hand that she remembered why he had so easily claimed her.

'All that's irrelevant. Let's just say revenge is a fine aphrodisiac.'

'Yes, but Elphick,' she protested, as his hands came round from behind her, removing the mirror, unbuttoning her blouse, his head buried in her neck, digging in, nipping it. 'It's so very unwise. We're colleagues.'

'You're just the presenter,' he said. 'I'm the producer. I could have you taken off the programme if I wanted to. That's aphrodisiac too.'

And so, it seemed it was.

'Yes, but Elphick,' she said, lying on his bed, naked. 'What about afterwards? Do you plan for me to be like Alice?'

'No such luck,' he said. 'I have no plans for afterwards.'

All the same, there was something she didn't understand. 'Yes, but Elphick,' she complained, before the dizziness of gratification silenced her altogether, and thankfully – so long, it seemed, since her body had managed to silence her mind – 'yes, but Elphick, I don't understand your motives.'

He did not bother to reply, nor indeed did it seem appropriate for him to do so, but the question lay between them afterwards, unanswered, as they dressed and she drank coffee and prepared to go home. There had been some element of calculation, of seduction in their encounter, and Isabel could not quite be sure whether it was in her, or him.

She collected Jason from Jennifer, and apologised for being late.

164

'Where's Homer?' asked Jason, in the bath. 'Where's Daddy?'

'He had to go away for a day or two,' she replied.

The explanation seemed to satisfy him. He did not ask for detail.

'I liked it round at Jennifer's,' he said. 'We had white bread and butter and little cakes with green icing.'

Green icing! Food-colouring agents were suspect; carcinogenic. At home Jason ate only the palest of pale foods. Isabel suddenly and violently missed Homer. Her crotch, agreeably sore and stiff, became an enduring reproach to her, outsmarting even her damaged eye. Of course Jason was Homer's child, by right and consent, if not by detail of birth. Ridiculous for anyone to suppose otherwise: unforgivable of her to have voiced her own doubts.

She sat beside Jason's bed while he fell asleep. She remembered the days when she had been handed on from one rich man to another, on loan, or in trust, or by reason of friendship, and thought perhaps they were better, simpler days than these. She longed for Homer to return – to forgive her; to restore her love for him; to seal up the ragged edges of her life, wrapping up past, present and future neatly and securely.

22

'I knew she'd been with a man,' said Jennifer. 'You can always tell when mothers are up to something. They dump their child on you, are late collecting, and are over-affectionate when they do.'

Spitter-spat. The rain has started up again. A few of us in Wincaster Row are mismatched, would start again with someone else if we could, but for reasons of decency, loyalty, habit and laziness stay where we are, and as we are. Besides, there are the children to consider, and in Wincaster Row we do a great deal of considering the children. Even Hilary, in her own way, considers them, and believes she is helping them by trying to abolish fatherhood. Hope says she never wants to have children. She would be a rotten mother, she says, and not having them is her way of looking after their interests. Her attitude upsets Jennifer, who defines woman as pre-mother, mother or ex-mother. Hope says there must surely be more to being alive than simply passing life on, and Jennifer replies bleakly – no.

Hilary, while viewing the male sex as an attack, feels she has a right to enjoy sexual intercourse with men, and is angry if she doesn't. She complains a good deal about men touching her up, at Wincaster Row street parties, Sunday lunch drinks and barbecues, and so forth, but Jennifer swears Hilary just imagines it. She's watched closely, and not a single male hand has been laid on Hilary's bosom, or tweaked her bottom. Yet was Jennifer watching *all* the time? We can't be sure. Perhaps men do touch up Hilary, in the same way as cats always sit on the laps of those who are least fond of them. Hope says, on the other hand, that she likes men touching her. Jennifer says all her husband has to do is touch her and she's pregnant. It is amazing that we all get on so well, since our experience of the same event is not only so diverse but produces such a variety of reaction.

As for marital infidelity, Jennifer says she daresay she would if she could, did not time, health and opportunity conspire against it. Hilary says her own marriage doesn't count but she would never go with a married man, for her sisters' sakes. But if men are of so little value, interjects Jennifer, wouldn't you be doing their wives a *favour*? Hilary turns pink with fury. Hope says she likes sleeping with married men – it's more exciting and there's no fear of a boring permanent relationship. She feels the freedom to fornicate is the greatest freedom of all, and she would be a Trotskyite or a Maoist or even a Stalinist, if only their views on sexual morality were not so old-fashioned and stern.

'But don't you feel guilt?' asks Jennifer, pink in turn; but no, Hope doesn't. Her desires are like some mighty meandering river – apparently casual, slipping silent through jungle land, but totally unstoppable.

I was unfaithful to Laurence during my sighted days. How old-fashioned the term seems now. But he was away a good deal, after all, and our relationship seemed to require me to provide him with clean shirts rather than sustain a vision of the perfectibility and permanence of love, which is natural to the young; and is, perhaps, a definition of innocence. I find it more difficult to betray him now that I can no longer look him in the eye. Fidelity seems desirable now that it is no longer owed to a seen object, a human being; but exists apart, in the head. I service this bright new blind concept as an aproned girl might service a vending machine. I feed in the raw ingredients – integrity and dependence and trust – and fidelity pours out, hot, steaming and plentiful, and Laurence clasps me and I clasp him, and that is all either of us needs.

Spitter-spat. Supposing one day my sight comes back? There is no reason, they say, why it should not. But what then? I do not quite feel equal to the responsibility of being whole and perfect. You can be lonelier sighted than flailing about in the dark.

Spitter-spat.

23

'I'm not convinced we have any major problem here,' said Harry McSwain, to Pete and Joe. 'By the time the husband returns she'll have learnt her lesson. Best thing he could have done was to go. A wife confesses; a husband reacts badly. She's learned the wisdom of keeping her mouth shut: normal life will presently resume. What did Tennyson have to say on this subject?'

And he leafed through his little red bound volume of the major works of Tennyson, and Pete and Joe marvelled at the character and nature of those who wielded power and influence in the world. Pete's wife, who now went to literature classes, had recently tried to explain it to her husband. 'It's ideas, Pete,' she'd said. 'Everything's ideas. They even say now the Bible isn't God's law but just a collection of poems.' He nodded politely, unbelieving, and wished first that she'd call him 'Kitten' more often, and second that she'd give up literature classes. He thought that under their influence she was neglecting her personal hygiene. She no longer seemed to fade into picturedom, framed between drapes; she went on existing when he wasn't looking. She wore long skirts, against his express wishes, and sometimes even had a vaguely hippy look, reminding him of Vera. Poor, limp, long, dirty Vera, who had had to go.

'Sir,' protested Pete now, 'with great respect, I repeat we have a major problem here. We know everything that goes on in that household, thanks to modern surveillance techniques, and we have done what we can, but it is not enough. We can cope with innuendo – in fact we have already dealt with one fairly severe threat from that direction but this is fact.'

'Ah yes,' said McSwain. 'Your girl who claimed the Candidate was impotent. Hard to believe, knowing Dandy.'

'She kissed and told once too often,' said Joe, with some satisfaction.

'Let me make one thing clear,' said McSwain. 'What you guys do to protect the Candidate is your business. We have a lot of money invested here. And not just money, it goes without saying, but the hopes and aspirations of the major part of America, who wish to live in dignity, prosperity and freedom, and with faith in the integrity of their leaders. Sometimes we may have to play it a little tough. That's why you boys are hired and rest assured you'll get every back-up you require. Nevertheless, I have to point out to you we are in a very delicate area in regard to Ms Rust, and I will need more persuading of the truth of what you say.'

'Sir,' said Pete, 'we have been in constant touch with the IFPC team of psychologists; they reckon Ms Rust to be in a fragile psychological state, which may presently crack wide open; and I repeat, innuendo is one thing but fact is another; we cannot have a woman claiming in public that her child is son to the President of the United States.'

'Let me look at that photograph again,' said McSwain, and

he took a magnifying glass to Jason's school photograph. Mrs Pelotti beamed in the background. Jason stood next to her.

'Why is that woman's hand on the child's neck?' he asked.

'He's quite a handful, sir,' said Joe, 'like his pa.'

They all smiled.

'If she chooses to say it,' said McSwain, 'I have to agree. No one's going to deny it. No doubt about it, the resemblance is strong.'

'Sir,' said Pete, choosing his moment wrongly, 'if the child were out of the way, the mother could be left. All kinds of accidents can happen to kids.'

'I did not hear that,' said McSwain, when he had recovered his wrath. 'The IFPC does not wage war on children. And that's the President's son you're talking about. A prince among men.'

He could see that this argument, though convincing to himself, might not weigh sufficiently heavily with Pete and Joe. They frightened him; he thought perhaps he, Frankenstein, had created twin monsters. There had been other means of silencing Vera: men could ensure women's loyalty in any number of ways. They had chosen death because they liked it.

'The time may come when the child is useful,' he said, and they understood that.

'Sir,' said Pete, 'I want your permission to act fast in relation to the mother. Soon she will realise she is in actual physical danger. Her move then will surely be to protect the child and herself by announcing the truth to the world, or at any rate the British public, and that's going to make worldwide headlines.'

'Martha Mitchell tried that before Watergate,' said

McSwain. 'Martha the Mouth. No one listened. They locked her up in a home for alcoholics.'

'Liddy would put her across his knee and jab her full of barbiturates,' said Pete, 'to render her comatose for twenty-four hours. It was all they could do.'

'Forgotten heroines of the women's movement,' said Joe.

'Sir,' said Pete, 'we have a clear duty to Pippa to make sure that kind of unpleasantness doesn't occur. A man must be free to live in a world where his past is not held against him. It seems a very basic right to me.'

He thought McSwain would understand that kind of talk, and indeed McSwain resorted to poetry, as he often did when he felt he'd lost a point.

'Poor Ms Rust,' he said. 'I do believe she loved him. What use to a woman is life when love is dead? When a man's love has failed her.

> Her tears fell with the dews at even;
> Her tears fell ere the dews were dried;
> She could not look on the sweet heaven,
> Either at morn or eventide. . . .
> She only said, "The night is dreary,
> He cometh not," she said;
> She said, "I am aweary, aweary,
> I would that I were dead!"'

From which Pete and Joe understood that they had made their point, and had permission to do what they felt they had to do, and were gratified.

But at that moment Dandy, idly playing back tapes in the Penthouse, sipping a forbidden bourbon and water, nibbling salt biscuits (a double crime – vastly increasing both sodium and calorie intake) happened to overhear the conversation. He broke security (that is the kind of effect alcohol has) lifted up the phone, got through to McSwain's office and said, 'What the holy shit is going on down there?'

24

Isabel roamed her empty house. The emptiness was of course in her and not in the house, which was as full of pot plants and wellington boots as ever. Nor was she alone. Jason was there, singing and blowing on a trumpet unkindly given for Jason's birthday by the Humbles in Wales, whose little daughters Jason had upset. But the presence of the child, however noisy, does not count as company to the desolate parent. Only at night, when the body of the child is warm against the mother's, does it become a source of comfort – greater even than the husband's who, though there by prior right, was only invited in in the first place, out of a cold, exciting, spouseless past – as an act of will and not of fate.

But by day, to the resentful and sulking parent, the child is an added source of exacerbation; a taker-away of strength and not giver of relief. The mother snaps, the child whines: there is no relief for the one or the other.

'For Christ's sake,' shouted lovely, kind, intelligent Isabel, the maker of a hundred egg-box castles, the putter-up of child art on the walls. 'Shut up, Jason!'
'You shut up,' shrieked Jason. 'I hate you. I'll cut you up

and put you in the dustbin, and they'll take you away and I'll never see you again.'

And the surveillance device in the kitchen ceiling heard all, and recorded all – much the same, no doubt, as once the all-seeing eye of God, which knew the innermost heart of man, and particularly woman – had recorded all, in the great Book of Judgement, to hold it against the sinner on Judgement Day.

Isabel looked at Jason and betrayed him in her heart, thinking, 'If you had never been born, I would not be in this trouble now. I would have my husband and my self-respect and my freedom to follow my own desires.'

That these wants and needs were contradictory she did not, could not, bother to consider. Anxiety and passion and anger consumed her; and indeed the conviction, unjustified by any evidence and no doubt the product of projection – that is, what I do, I think you do too – the conviction that Homer had run off with another woman and was at that very moment lying in some seamy bed. The vision of the bed she held in her mind was remarkably like the bed on which she had so lately lain with Elphick, but that did not occur to Isabel.

Isabel took Jason to school.
'No Homer?' enquired Mrs Pelotti.
'He's away on business,' said Isabel. 'A neighbour will be collecting him.'
'So long as we know,' said Mrs Pelotti. 'We don't hand over our children to strangers. You do have a nasty black eye!'

175

'Don't I just?' said Isabel.

I should, thought Isabel on the way home through littered streets, have done what any sensible woman would have done: not given birth to Dandy's child. And perhaps, in the subdued anger of yesterday, I had been right. Perhaps she did not love Homer at all, and never had; perhaps necessity and despair had mixed and registered themselves as love. And if she didn't love Homer, didn't love her husband, then indeed, as she had glimpsed yesterday, momentarily, as the naked Elphick advanced upon her, then a whole new wonderful world opened up, in which permission to love had not been all swallowed up but stretched ahead, a glittery stream of emotion, pleasure and excitement.

But if she didn't love Homer then why did she feel this angry, hungry, gnawing pain, just because he was not there, had left without permission? Why did the stream of freedom run so icy cold?

Isabel telephoned Dr Gregory.
'It's better if you telephone between ten to the hour and the hour,' he said. 'Otherwise I'm with a patient and not in a position to answer. Fortunately I had a cancellation; that is the only reason I picked up the telephone. Is something the matter?'
'Yes,' said Isabel.
'You cancelled the last appointment,' he said, fretfully.
'I'm sorry,' she said, which seemed to satisfy him, as if expressions of regret in his patients were rare. He agreed to see her the following morning at his Harley Street surgery.
'I expect it will wait until then,' he said.

'I may of course be dead,' said Isabel.

'Is that a suicide threat?' he asked.

'No,' she said.

'In that case, unless someone is planning to murder you, I expect you'll make it through until tomorrow.'

Murder!

Isabel went briskly round to see Maia next door. Her emotional turmoil subsided as a boiling pan of milk subsides when someone throws in a spoonful of cold water. Her head, announcing danger, had ruthlessly thrust aside all matters of the heart, as if personal desolation, confusion and a sense of loss were merest luxuries, all very well in peace but hardly in war.

'Maia,' said Isabel. 'Something comes to mind. The fate of President Sukarno's mistress. Some said she was a piano teacher, others a nightclub performer. Enough that she had the President's child; she lived in Manila. But when the boy was six she started asking for money; recognition for both of them. Mother and child were promptly killed in a car crash. And that would have been that, except questions were asked about the accident, and the President's men tried to frame her brother, who always knew more than he should anyway. But the frame didn't stick, the Press got to know, the brother was saved. The President, probably incidentally, was assassinated; but that of course didn't help mother and child. They were dead. What lesson do we learn from that, Maia?'

'That it's better to live in the West, not the East,' said Maia.

'It might be,' said Isabel, 'that when male power and prestige is at stake the lives and happiness of women and children are immaterial. That women just have to learn to dodge bombs, napalm, defoliant and so forth, while getting on with their daily lives. It doesn't seem good enough to me.'

'She could just have kept quiet,' said Maia. 'If she hadn't asserted herself she'd still be alive today.'

'And I have to keep quiet on my programme,' said Isabel. 'I have to talk about coloured honey and flood barriers while the world crumbles about us. I am a tame woman, Maia. A kept female pet: I open my mouth and say what most pleases and least offends.'

'It isn't your programme,' Maia pointed out. 'It's theirs. You're only there by courtesy.'

'Of course, once they described her as a nightclub performer, the world turned its back. That meant she was a prostitute and prostitutes are more animal than human; they can be slaughtered with impunity. They are devoured while still alive, that's all. Only she had the President's child, and so she couldn't quite be dismissed. She had a womb, and it worked; and she carried the President's power within her, and brought it to life, and there was even a rumour she taught the piano – that patiently and quietly she made the world a better place. And it so confused everyone she had to go.'

'I imagine she was just a political inconvenience,' said Maia.

'It was more than that,' said Isabel.

'Or perhaps she asked for too much money. We'll never know. No doubt it seemed important to everyone at the time; but now Sukarno's regime, for good or bad, is swept away. No one remembers.'

'I remember her,' said Isabel. 'And the President's child. The hope of the present and the hope of the future.'

She looked at her watch.

'I'll have to ask Jennifer to collect Jason,' she said. 'Yet again. It's supposed to be Homer's turn today, but where is he? Fairness and equality in marriage are hard to achieve. It's all right on a rational day, but so few of them are.'

'The most important thing,' said Maia, 'is to stay alive.'

'I know that,' said Isabel, smiling her broken smile, her black eye gleaming. 'I'm working on it.'

25

Dandy Ivel paced to and fro, hands behind his back, shoulders lowered, head forward. So little Jason walked. Jason, in London, walked and watched Popeye on television; Dandy watched other flickering images on a screen – of Elphick plunging into Isabel, rearing over her. The film ran too fast, the element of caricature was extreme. Even so, when Isabel cried out, and Dandy had not made her do it, Dandy suffered.

'We've seen enough,' said McSwain. Dandy was pink and perspired. McSwain worried about Dandy's blood pressure; the candidate lingered on the verge, always, of hypertension and although normal sexual activity always seemed to help bring his body back to health, sexual activity allied to emotional distress made matters worse. Dandy's heart pumped, the blood raced, the arteries fought back; the battles of the mind, the great war between achievement and peace, each finding their allies in the body, wreaking its eventual destruction. This, for McSwain, had been a difficult decision to make – choosing between what Dandy had to know and what Dandy would prefer not to know. Easier if Dandy backed out altogether from the decision-making process; but the time was not yet ripe for that.

And the hypertension was not yet severe enough to constitute any kind of physical threat: only a political one, if rumours got about. He took care to underplay the problem, even to Pete and Joe.

'We've seen enough,' repeated McSwain, but no one instructed the projectionist to stop the film. The images fascinated. Elphick rested; began again.

'Why do you show me this?' Dandy demanded. 'What good does it do? It's an interference with the fundamental rights of the individual to privacy and a decent life.'

'Sir,' said Pete, 'a) they are neither of them American citizens, and b) she is not living a decent life. We have a forcible demonstration of that here before us today.'

'I guess she lives like anyone else,' said Dandy.

'Not like the majority of American mothers and daughters, sir, who put their trust in you,' said Pete.

McSwain shook his head at Pete, who fell silent.

Isabel moved on top of Elphick, head fallen back, neck stretched. Dandy knew well enough what his team wanted. They wanted to run Isabel out of his soul, as they had run her out of his mind. He had let her body go, for the sake of a vision in which she could play no possible part. Now he must let the memory of her go, and with that the notion that love and power, man and woman, earth and fire, could somehow be reconciled. He must split Pippa Dee from out of her mould, shiny and new and man-made, dust her down, and make do with that. There was no reason, looking now at Isabel, to believe that he had been central in her life, as she had been in his.

'All the same,' he said to no one in particular, 'she kept the baby. She didn't destroy it.'

181

'She kept it to nail a man,' said Joe, 'so far as she was concerned, and may Mary forgive her for it.'
'The kid dumped on neighbours, too,' said Pete. 'I never thought she'd stoop as low as that.'

Dandy groaned. Superman and Lois, soaring through outer space, to the music of the cosmos, come to this?

'Do what you want,' he said. 'Do what you have to.'
'God willing,' said McSwain after Dandy had left, 'we won't have to take extreme measures. But we must be empowered to use them, should the need arise.'
'That's my point entirely,' said Pete.

Dandy went straight out and chatted up the projectionist's girlfriend, who was dizzy with desire in the projection room, the kind of urgent, automatic lust which pornographic images create, and which her boyfriend – in any case more accustomed to them than she – was too busy and too proud to satisfy.

Dandy took her to the Ladies' Room and barred the door by wedging a little fawn brocade chair beneath its handle. She did not demur, but stripped off with enthusiasm. She was flattered. Her boyfriend had not objected: this was the Candidate, after all, and he was honoured by proxy. Dandy laid her down on the fawn nylon carpet, between glittery mirror-lined walls, and finally subdued the ghost of Isabel. Sex was good, and girls were grand, and oblivion desirable. He erased Isabel from his mind as a nervous typist erases a mistake; over and over and over, long after the need has gone and the original error forgotten, and left her to her fate.

'We have a problem here,' said Pete to Joe, waiting outside, embarrassed, as members of the IFPC staff, some of them senior, went unnecessarily up and down the corridor. Some of them laughed or grinned. Amazing how quickly word got round.

'We certainly do,' said Joe to Pete.

26

Snuffle-snuffle. Before I lost my sight I'd snuffle too, weeping my eyes out up and down Wincaster Row, asking advice, proclaiming resentments, red-eyed and self-pitying, as a result of some slight or other offered by Laurence, claiming the company and help of the neighbours as my right.

'I wish you wouldn't,' Laurence would say when peace and amity were restored. 'My mother never did it. She kept things to herself. She had her pride. Her loyalty was all to her husband, no matter how he behaved.'
'She died of cancer. It ate away inward instead of out-ward.'
'There is no evidence whatsoever that cancer and discretion are linked,' he said haughtily; but it seems as good a theory as any other.

Oddly, now I have lost my sight, I no longer offer my life to friends and neighbours. They offer theirs to me. I have gained in dignity; or perhaps it is that they cannot do for me what I can do for them – penetrate the blackness of despair with shafts of light. Nor can I see their flushed cheeks and puffy eyes and runny noses. I hear their voices, though – streams of sound running in and out of the fabric of life in Wincaster Row, threading through the fuchsia bush, twining in and out of the railings of the communal garden: mingling with laughter and endearments.

Oh pity me, help me, look after me. I am only a child, not fit to be out on my own! No one understands me. Everyone ill-treats me. Especially him; especially her; the one in all the world I thought was perfect, the only one I trusted. Now I see what he has done, listen to what she said. Is there any forgiving it? How can I be expected to live with such insults in such an atmosphere?

See, he tore up my wedding photographs! See, she has a lover! She's turning the children against me! He bribes them, doesn't really love them! And we hoped for so much: for us, for us, it was meant to be different.

Yes, and for me too. Snuffle, snuffle in the dark, where no one can approach me, not even Laurence, somewhere too deep in my being for him to reach.

Snuffle, snuffle. Oliver has a cold. I hear him sneezing even before I hear his footstep. Oliver the architect from No. 13. His wife Anna takes the children at weekends. He looks after them during the week. Her absence is temporary, or so she says. Anna has fallen in love: she wants time to work it out in her lover's bed, while Oliver makes the breakfast porridge and fishes out grey school socks from under the boys' beds, and school ties from behind the bookcases. He pays for the children's education – Anna says they have to have all possible advantages, their home life being so disrupted.

'Why shouldn't he look after them?' Hilary asks. 'They're

185

his children as much as hers. If he wasn't prepared to look after them he should never have had them.'

Oliver usually has a cold. He weeps with his nose instead of with his eyes. He loves his wife, who wonders if she loves him, and so presumably does not – and sneezes and blows and wipes. *Snuffle-snuffle*.

'Just when we were so cosy,' complains Hilary this afternoon, 'and really rapping, here comes a man and spoils everything.'

Here comes a man! Hilary's great-grandpapa hit her great-grandmama with a poker and killed her. Hilary's grandmother was there. Now there's an event – a great boulder tumbling into the river of time, and diverting the flow into untoward and meaner channels. Such events take generations to wear away, dissolve. Here comes a man! She had ten children and didn't want eleven: if she'd had only nine Hilary wouldn't have existed at all.

We contemplate this fact up and down Wincaster Row and shake our heads over it, wondering how we can wish ourselves out of existence, since our very being depends on so much sin and sorrow, and all things we would do away with if we could.

'Sit down quietly and listen, Oliver,' says Jennifer, 'but not too near in case we catch your cold.'
'It's a psychosomatic cold,' said Oliver, 'not the catching kind. What's the story?'
'It's Maia's fantasy about Homer and Isabel from No. 3,' says Hope.

'There was a story at one time,' observed Oliver, 'that the child wasn't Homer's but Dandy Ivel's.'

'Maia,' says Hope in astonishment. 'This story isn't *true*?'

'Yes,' I reply.

Snuffle-snuffle. It will require an intensity of entertainment to take Oliver's mind off his wife and her lover. When she takes the children on Sundays she sits them in front of the video while she retires with her lover to the bedroom. The worse she treats the boys, Oliver complains, the more they seem to love her. There's no justice in the world.

27

Isabel lay down, as requested by Dr Gregory, on a shiny leather couch. Harley Street traffic rumbled below. She preferred his St John's Wood rooms. There she could feel interesting, and pleasantly neurotic: here, by association, she became a patient, and in need of cure.

'I'd rather sit,' she said. 'Why do I have to lie down? Does it symbolise my submission?'

'Why don't you like lying down?' It was his habit to respond to questions by asking more. His chair was placed at the head of the couch, so she could not see him.

'You might attack me.'

'Do you often fear attack?'

'Yes.'

'Just from me or from all quarters?'

'From all quarters. Does that mean I feel guilty?'

'Do you feel guilty?'

'Yes.'

'Why?'

'Because I committed adultery. Does the word sound dramatic? I'm sorry. It was the word my mother used to describe my father's actions. Your father? Oh, he committed adultery. As if that negated him utterly.'

'So now you are negated?'

'No. I feel rather good about it.'

'Why did it seem so urgent to get in touch with me? You must only call me between ten to the hour and the hour: I think I told you that.'

'Because there's something wrong and I can't put my finger on it. My home doesn't feel like my home, or Homer like my husband.'

'But Jason feels like your child?'

'Mine and Dandy's.'

She could feel him smiling.

'Do you think I made him up?' She was angry.

'I think that until we have had a few more sessions you should try to live your life more quietly. If you have fantasies about the parentage of your child keep them to yourself. Keep out of the beds of your colleagues if you possibly can. Do not give credence to your own feelings of omnipotence – that the world is yours for the saving. It isn't. Psychotherapy stirs up many things: it's meant to. Emotions and defences, in neurotic patients, have been wrongly laid down, as if a pattern in a tiled floor has gone wrong. The tiles must be disturbed, re-sorted, re-aligned and set back down again in a proper pattern. While the floor's up – tread softly! That's the art. You seem to have been clumping round in rather large boots, Ms Rust, kicking as you go.'

Isabel was silent for some time.

Dr Gregory did not break the silence.

'I see,' she said presently. 'I never had a proper home in the beginning, so I don't feel entitled to one now. I never had a father, so part of me thinks I'd better not have a husband. That's why they don't feel real. I am unconsciously

189

trying to get rid of Homer. I am ambivalent towards him. Part of me feels I'm too good for him, I'm busy denying him. I won't let him be Jason's father. I don't want him to be. So I invented the whole Dandy incident. Because I remember it doesn't mean it happened. I am lying here on a psychiatrist's couch in Harley Street, and I am quite, quite mad.'

'Mad is probably overstating it,' he said, kindly.

'Homer tried to suggest all this to me but I wouldn't listen. I was set on naming an alternative father, and Dandy Ivel fitted the bill very well.'

'Right.' Dr Gregory gave what she assumed was a laugh, a little *skwark*, like a hen cut off mid-cackle.

'So what happens now? Does delusion evaporate? Do I look at Jason and see Homer in his eyes, not Dandy? When Homer's cold body enters mine, do I stop remembering Dandy's warmth?'

'You experience Homer as cold?' It seemed to interest him.

'If I said so I expect I do.'

'Body temperature hardly varies from one person to another. It must be purely subjective. Poor Homer.'

'Yes,' said Isabel. 'Poor Homer.'

'When you feel paranoia coming on,' said Dr Gregory, 'for that is what you are suffering from, and very disagreeable it is too, put up with the symptoms as you would a physical pain: wait for them to pass. They will.'

'I'm almost convinced,' said Isabel. 'Except other people see the likeness to Dandy Ivel in Jason. What about this? I've heard them say so.'

'You think you've heard them,' he said. 'It may be just the form your voices take.'

'Have I really got a black eye?' she asked.

'Oh yes.' Again the cut-off cackle. 'You've certainly got that.'

'And Homer did it?'

'I should think so. I'd have hit you, I expect, in similar circumstances.'

'It may mean I can't present the programme tomorrow.'

'I would have thought,' said Dr Gregory, unfeelingly, 'that that was the least of your worries.'

She was late fetching Jason from school. The last straggle of children and mothers came down the street as she arrived. Inside, there was no sign of Jason, in the cloakroom, or in his classroom. She called his name, with increasing panic, into echoing empty rooms and corridors.

'Jason! Jason!' Her heart froze with terror.

Child art mocked her from the walls; unfinished sums from desks. A guinea pig, part of a learning-to-love programme, snuffled in a quiet room. 'Jason! Jason!'

Mrs Pelotti, in orange cloak and flying hair, swept down the corridor.

'Mrs Rust, what are you doing? School's long over.'

'I've lost Jason. I can't find Jason.'

'Your neighbour collected him. You told me she would this morning. What *is* the matter with you?'

She gave Isabel sherry out of the medicine cupboard.

'In any case,' said Mrs Pelotti, 'you were very late. I would have been very cross if poor little Jason had been kept waiting. As it is, no harm's done.'

'I hope you won't put me down on Jason's record,' enquired Isabel, 'as a neurotic mother?'

'If I did,' Mrs Pelotti replied, 'it would be for Jason's sake, not as a rebuke to you. I'm quite sorry for mothers these days. They have lost their children to the nation's education system. I quite often find them roaming the school, looking for children they fancy they've lost who are perfectly safe somewhere else. But I'm very tired, and rather fanciful.'

Isabel found Jason in Jennifer's house, watching television. 'I got him to sit down and watch,' said Jennifer, 'instead of roaming up and down as usual. I know that always annoys you, though I can't think why it does.'

28

Pete went to visit a certain Dr Alcott, who lived in a pleasant home in Georgetown. Dr Alcott was an English expatriate, wrote books on popular psychiatry, and was in a perpetual state of war with the medical establishment, whom he liked to accuse of ritual thinking and cowardice in the face of chemotherapy. Dr Alcott's voice boomed; the neighbours could hear his denunciations, and the paintings on his walls shook. They were mostly of elephants, for whom he had a liking: slow, sensible beasts.

Pete dressed up as a journalist. That is to say, he took off his tie and unbuttoned a shirt not designed to be worn tieless. He borrowed his wife's brother's shoes, which were of suede, and did not shave before he left the house or brush and buff his nails.

'I wish you looked like that more often,' said his wife, as he went out the front door. That upset him. Her hair was cut short and bristled all over her head. She'd had a smooth and shiny hairstyle before, though he would have been at a loss to describe it, either now or then. He said as much. He'd liked that, hated this.
'Oh Pete,' she'd said. 'That's it! You never see what you

193

think is normal, only what to you is abnormal. And you're out of step with the rest of the world. I wish you'd realise it. Can't you get a different job?'

That didn't help, either. He had always thought of himself as a happily married man.

Pete told Dr Alcott he was writing an article on the place of sexual offenders in modern society. He offered to pay a research fee but Dr Alcott declined to accept one.

'Knowledge is free,' shouted the doctor. 'I accept payment for making the ill healthy, because a money transaction speeds the healing process. That's about the only thing the Viennese doctor got right.'

'The Viennese doctor?'

'Freud!'

'I see.'

'For Freud read Fraud! Bunch of European crazies! They're no better today. They think they've got depression licked. They put up the Indoleamine Hypothesis: they think the root of all trouble is too much tryptophan buzzing about in the brain. I'm a catecholamine man myself: it's norepinephrine which does it – that's a breakdown of tyrosine. You follow me? They're dosing their depressives with what cures maniacs. Follow me?'

'Sure, sure,' said Pete, busily writing on a journalist's pad, borrowed from his wife.

'Take a healthy, normal animal like an elephant. What keeps it so sane? Its brain. Elephants' brains don't produce morephrine. And no one can say elephants copulate like rabbits. Follow?'

'Sure. So what cures sexual mania? Tricyclics? Are they the treatment?'

'Yes. Desipramine, Imipramine, Nortriptyline.'

'Long words,' remarked Pete.

'That's to keep the relatives quiet. What hope do they have? They're people, not chemists. Every patient these days is a living clinical laboratory. And why not? Loonies aren't people. The relatives keep forgetting that.'

'Now tell me,' said Pete, 'how State Penitentiaries treat sexual offenders.'

'Neuroleptics,' said Dr Alcott. 'They're the major tranquillisers. Chloropramazine is popular in quelling the urgent phallus. So's Halperidol. I like Halperidol myself.'

'Contra-indications?' asked Pete.

'They can bring the blood pressure down too low, if the patient's that way inclined. Dizziness, nausea, fainting. I like to give Halperidol in conjunction with Lithium, which raises the blood pressure, just in case.'

'Lithium?'

'Lithium Carbonate. Wonder drug. Gone out of favour. Everyone's bored with it. Name's too simple.'

'Is it safe?'

'Of course. For any ordinary red-blooded American just going over the top, proving his manhood once or twice too often for his wife's convenience. Tastes okay too. She should crumble it in the soup. Sometimes I think my wife's giving me a tricyclic. I get headaches – feel dizzy – something's wrong with my hearing. Do I shout?'

'What's the dosage?'

'Which? Halperidol?'

'With Lithium?'

'Three hundred milligrams a day. Of each. That's what I'm on. My wife doesn't like sex, you see.'

His voice rose to let the neighbours know.

'I don't blame her, of course,' he added, more softly. 'Look at me!'

195

His belly wobbled; his face was puffy.

'No impairment of the intellectual faculties?' enquired Pete.

'Good God no! Look at me!' His hands trembled as he opened the door with an unnatural jerky motion.

Probably too high a dosage, thought Pete. If Dandy starts doing that all we have to do is lower the intake.

Joe contacted a chemist who made up Halperidol and Lithium into effervescent tablets, which were pretty much identical in flavour and appearance to the Vitamin C tablets Dandy took morning and night. Pippa Dee had persuaded him to do this. Dandy respected and admired Pippa, but neither loved her nor lusted after her: she had no need to fear his satyriasis, if that was what it was. Joe and Pete liked to think Pippa was on their side. Dandy had cut down his drinking for Pippa's sake, not because the IFPC had told him to.

When he was President they would be married. It would be like Prince Charles and Lady Di, and a second, a third, a fourth term inevitable. And after that a Monarchy; a Succession.

Failure entered no one's head but Dandy's.

It was McSwain who was impatient now.

'Get the hell over there,' he said, 'to the other side of the Atlantic. Find out what's going on. There are too many folks over there, and over here for that matter, collecting a salary for sweet eff-all.'

Pete and Joe got. They were allowed to travel Concorde, since time, McSwain said, was of the essence, and that pleased them. Their weapons, properly checked and accounted for to Security, travelled separately, in the baggage hold, which made them feel naked and strange.

29

Listen! A leaf rustles in the dark, a twig breaks. Something prowls out there in the forest. *Patter-patter*. It's a sabre-toothed tiger, without a doubt. The fire is dying in the entrance of the cave. Children sleep in a pile in the ashes maimed, dirty, wild. The women huddle together, gibbering with fear. Where are the men?

'I'll tell you where the men are,' says Hilary. 'They're all dead drunk from chewing betel nuts, or out awarding each other bits of stone for bravery in the face of the mammoth, or in the next cave killing other men's women and children.'

'Look here!' says Oliver. 'I'm a man. I don't kill women and children.'
'Except for one or two of the men,' adds Hilary unkindly, 'too crippled by love or lust to join the gang.'

Patter-patter. Danger approaches. It's real, too. It isn't games: hand over hand, as children like to play in front of the fire, your hand, my hand, faster and faster, men and women, your point, my point. Outside it's dark and cold; so cold it will freeze you to death. Men's hands are bigger, stronger.

Thump! Your finger's broken.

'I wonder what cavewomen did when their periods came on,' says Jennifer. 'If you'll excuse such menstrual talk, Oliver.'
'Don't apologise like that, Jennifer,' says Hilary, furious. 'Don't be coy.'
'Nothing,' says Hope. 'They did what girls do in this country if they're shut up in punishment cells in prisons or mental homes. They just bleed all over everything. You wear a stiff canvas shift – no underwear. You stay in your cell twenty-four hours a day. There's nothing in the cell except you – and a toilet without a lid. No toilet paper. Food is pushed through a hole in the door three times a day. You're taken out for a bath once a week. If you start bleeding in between, too bad. No one knows but you. You can batter and bang against the door but then you just stay in longer. So you do what cavewomen did. You just bleed, all over your legs and all over the floor.'

We all turn towards Hope in astonishment. She smiles brilliantly, gives her little careless laugh.
'I was in one,' she said. 'When I was fifteen I went peculiar. I used to steal and pick up men in the streets. I was remanded in custody, tried to escape, scaled a wall or two, delivered a punch or two; it was six months before my parents could get me out. I spent six weeks in a punishment cell. Just my luck to have two periods in that time.'

Oliver breaks the silence.
'But in men's prisons the conditions are the same,' he says.
'The men do have toilet paper in their quiet cells, I believe,' says Hope. 'Quiet cells! How nice it sounds.'

Patter-patter. Danger prowls. Lives are ruined. Hope chatters over the surface of her life, wide-eyed, wild-hearted, playing safe.

'I think your vision of gibbering, frightened women is unsound,' says Jennifer, briskly. 'They would have firewood gathered, and if they heard a sabre-toothed tiger they'd simply build up the fire. Others would have sharpened stakes ready to get its eyes if it pounced. The children wouldn't be piled up dirty and in the ashes, they'd be on proper clean beds of moss and straw, lying in rows inside the cave with their faces and hands wiped.'

Patter-patter. Listen! Jennifer lives in a state of siege, building up the fire, sharpening stakes in preparation for danger. She licks her children into shape, as a good mother cat licks her kittens. Do this, do that! Careful as you cross the road, don't talk to strange men, fluoride tablets to preserve from dental cavities. An apple and an orange and an egg for every child every day, building strong bones, firm flesh, smooth skin. Eight children in her household. An orange a day a head, over say, fifteen years. Forty thousand oranges or so, to be bought, carried home, prepared, peeled, wiped up after and the peel disposed of. All in search of Vitamin C.

Patter-patter. If there's nothing else to fear for the children, fear a cold in the nose.

I have no children, but I too suffer from fear; I wake in the night with a start, sure there's someone, something in the room. And I can't even turn on the light. So I invite the fear in, I speak to it: I say, tell me why you are so much greater than any individual fate could merit – and it replies, because I am all your fears; you are all one, you are not as many as you think you are: you must learn to share me. Loss suffered by any woman is every woman's loss. The voice of fear echoes in the dark, and I embrace it, and it melts into me, and is part of me, and is gone, and I fall back to sleep again, from black to darker black.

Nor do I believe that the sound of pattering ever stops: the soft insistences of fear outside the fire's light — just that from time to time I sleep, and can no longer hear it.

30

Homer, as everyone, including Elphick, Maia, Jennifer, Hope, Pete and Joe kept predicting, returned home soon enough.

He had not, after all, as only Hilary had assumed was the case, flung Isabel weeping and discarded into the great heaving marvellous maelstrom of Women Alone. No. Homer returned as Isabel slept, Jason beside her, and lifted her out of the strange new land of fear and self-determination with delicate male fingers, and placed her back into married respectability, on the pedestal of his and society's esteem. From this vantage point the view is clear and bright, and the sun shines in a well-intentioned perma-nent kind of way, on fixed mountain peaks of good behaviour and conventional morality.

No wonder so many want to dwell there, and fight to remain above the churning blades of sedition, revolution and sacrifice.

Isabel slept the sleep of the emotionally and sexually exhaus-ted, a heavy recuperative sleep which held no promise for the following day but reacted only to what had gone before.

Homer had to smooth her hair, whisper her name, shake her, before she would consent to wake.

'If I was an intruder, Isabel,' Homer said, reproachfully, 'you wouldn't have stood a chance.'
It was nearly one o'clock in the morning.
'They said you were in New York,' said Isabel.
'So I was,' he said. 'But I missed you. I came home.'
'Don't wake Jason,' said Isabel. She sat up, warm from sleep. He put his jacketed arms around her. He smelt of aircraft: a mixture of sweat and hygiene, perfume and machinery. Fleetingly, she thought of Dandy. Homer had not shaved. His chin was rough.
'Six-year-old boys shouldn't sleep with their mothers,' observed Homer. 'What would Dr Gregory say?'
'I don't know and I don't care,' said Isabel, although neither was true. She knew well enough what Dr Gregory would say, since he always put forward the most disagreeable and difficult propositions available; that she was betraying her maternal role, absorbing comfort rather than giving it, and thus confusing him. 'But I'll ask him tomorrow if you like. And while you've been away Jason hasn't wet the bed or bitten, so perhaps it's you who should be seeing him, not me.'

Homer laughed.
'Get him to iron the fantasies out of your life, Isabel, for all our sakes. I can't stand too much jet lag.'
'Why are you so cheerful?' she asked. 'I've been having a dreadful time.'
'Because it's funny, I suppose. You suddenly announcing Jason isn't mine. He so obviously is. I should never have taken it seriously. He looks like me, thinks like me, feels

like me. He certainly believes he's my son, and Isabel, it would instantly stop being funny if anything to the contrary were ever to get back to Jason and upset him.'

'Of course,' said Isabel. Time raced on, the child grew, twisted the strands of life into a new and unexpected pattern, colours growing in intensity, as the fabric of the mother's life faded and grew thin. She acquiesced. 'Of course,' said Isabel. 'He's your child.'

Homer scooped Jason up in his slight but steely arms and carried the sleeping child away from the confusion of the maternal bed into the tidiness of his own. Jason groaned and flailed a little, protesting, but did not fully wake.

'He's heavy,' said Homer.

Isabel quelled the thought that so, yes, Dandy was heavy, had lain heavily upon her, in mastery. Homer lay lightly, in partnership.

Homer undressed and slipped into bed beside her, pushing up her nightdress, feeling her breasts. She lay still and compliant and oddly wary, as if a sudden move might make him dangerous, make the fingers pinch and twist, and not caress. The hammer blows of his body in hers might race out of control, driving so forcibly as to destroy her. She depended, she understood it now, on his goodwill, and that was both sinister and precarious.

'Relax,' he said. 'Everything's all right. Everything's back to normal. Dr Gregory stirred up too much in you, that's all. It will subside again.'

He talks too much, she thought, for someone in the grip of passion. And my mind is cold too. Why?

'What's the matter?' he persisted.
'I'm so helpless,' she said. 'You could hurt me.'
'You must be feeling very guilty,' he said. 'So could you hurt me, when I'm open to you like this, but you don't. Of course you don't. Isabel, this is Homer!'

She thought of the list upon the kitchen wall: the life-sharing, the time-sharing, the chore-sharing. The joint determination to live in fairness and equity. Homer. She didn't want him. He was like a brother she didn't particularly get on with: too well known for erotic response.
'You've changed,' he said. 'Something's changed.'

She remembered Elphick. Elphick had been there, where now Homer went. She felt no guilt, only an increase in wariness.
'Nothing's changed,' she said. But it had.
Homer's face came and went above her. First near, then far. She almost laughed. When he was near she wanted him far; when he was far she was terrified in case he did not return. She felt the automatic response of her body, and for a time forgot reason. He was not Homer, nor Elphick, nor Dandy, nor Grimble, nor a dozen other men she could hardly remember: he was all of them, and he would do.

Homer slept, neatly and quietly. Isabel lay awake and for once envied her mother, and understood why she had let the painful and confused part of her atrophy, and how she could live for ever, dried up by the hot yellow sand, observing the workings of God from a safe distance, while her daughter floundered and moiled in the morass of her own emotions and ambitions and fears.

Next door, in Maia's house, a light went on. Perhaps she can't sleep, thought Isabel, and then realised it must be Laurence, not Maia, for Maia would not bother to flick the switch. Maia lived in the light of her own mind, since that was all she had. Isabel, conscious of a faint flutter of gratitude, like some unborn child within her, slept.

31

Homer took Jason to school on the back of his bicycle. 'Don't be late,' said Isabel, 'Mrs Pelotti is fussing.'
'Don't you be late picking him up,' said Homer, amiably, as they wobbled off into a slight fog. Jason laughed over his shoulder at his mother; he clasped his father with certainty, small hands interlacing on Homer's chest. Homer's son. Isabel waved goodbye and went back into her house.

Today was transmission day. She would rehearse from midday to three o'clock, return home, collect Jason at four from school, and leave again for the actual show at seven, by which time Homer would be back from work and able to look after Jason.

Everything was back to normal. Even her eye seemed better, the flesh less puffy, although still wonderfully discoloured. 'Christ, I'm sorry,' Homer had said. 'I certainly didn't mean to do that.'

The telephone rang as she shut the door behind the departing Homer and Jason. It was Doreen Humble from Wales.

'Isabel,' said Doreen, and Isabel imagined she could hear in the background the sound of snuffling livestock and coughing children, 'I was ringing up to see if you were okay, if you needed anything. You can always come down here and hide out until it's all over.'

'That's very good of you, Doreen. Until what's all over?'

'The election.'

'What election?'

'The Presidential election, of course.'

'But why should I, Doreen?'

'You mean you haven't seen it.'

'Seen what?'

'*Cosmopolitan.*'

'I don't read *Cosmopolitan*: I wouldn't have thought it was your style either.'

'It might yet be,' said Doreen, taking mild offence. 'You read it,' she went on. 'There's a feature on media couples, with you and Homer in it, and a nice picture of Jason. Turn over, and there's a double spread about Dandy Ivel, and Isabel, the likeness is unmistakable; it's most unfortunate. Couldn't they have stopped it? Isabel, is it *safe*? I don't suppose you want to talk about it, even though everyone else is. All I'm saying, is; if you want somewhere to hide, here we are. Only I suppose your phone's tapped – well, everyone's is – so now I've said it that's no good either.'

'Doreen,' said Isabel, carefully. 'When you say everyone's talking about it, who is? And what are they talking about?'

'Grimble's talking about it, propping up bars with it up and down Fleet Street. About you and your affair with Dandy Ivel and Jason being his son. You took his seat on Concorde's maiden flight and he's never forgiven it. The paper went to great lengths to get him seated next to Dandy. And you sent back all that phoney junk about Alabama when you were holed up with Dandy in an hotel. I shan't ask what it was like because that would be vulgar. But they do say he keeps trying but he's not much good at it. No one can say we're out of touch down here in Wales; we seem to know more about what's going on than you city folk. I wonder if *Cosmopolitan* juxtaposed those pictures by mistake, or was it someone's idea of a joke?'

'I'll ring you back, Doreen,' said Isabel. 'There's someone at the door.'

There wasn't of course, but she felt the need to sit down. Presently she called Dr Gregory at his home. A woman, presumably his wife, said he had just left for his Harley Street rooms.

'Give him a message from me,' said Isabel, 'when you see him. It's this. Just because you think people are persecuting you, it doesn't mean they aren't.'

'Very well,' said Mrs Gregory, dubiously. 'Just wait until I write that down.' And she presently repeated, 'Just because you think people are persecuting you, it doesn't mean they aren't.'

'Quite so,' said Isabel. 'Just tell him that. I'll be round to see him as soon as I can.'

Mixed with fear and anxiety, now, was the exhilaration of vindication. She'd been right; he'd been wrong. She was not suffering from guilt, paranoia, stress, sexual fantasies or obsession; she was more than the mere product of a troubled past, more than a dismal walking cluster of neuroses, obsessed by fake, pitiful and presumptuous memories, a source of danger and distress to her child and her husband – she was the mother of Dandy's son. She had loved Dandy in reality as well as in fantasy.

A key turned in the front door. She was frightened. She and Homer were the only people who had keys to the house – except for Jennifer, who kept one in case of accidents or inadvertently slamming doors. But Jennifer would ring, or knock, or call.

'Isabel!' It was Homer, returning with Jason. 'I had a puncture. They're new tyres, too. I don't understand it. Perhaps it's sabotage.'
'But now Jason's going to be late.'
'So am I.' He was cross. 'Ring the school, tell them he's on his way. They can't really object. Call me a taxi: you'd better take him round.'

Isabel made both phonecalls and set out with Jason for school: she took the shortest but not the safest route. Mrs Pelotti would be cross – Jason kept saying so. She held his hand tightly. She too felt, now, suddenly, that Jason was invested with some special importance; that she was his protector as well as his mother. During the day she would work out what to do – what the best course of action was. Perhaps an approach to Dandy herself, with the assurance of her silence and discretion? Forgetting Grimble – if they could, or would. That was the obvious, feminine, cowardly thing to do. To render herself passive, invisible, agreeable. Thus she and Jason could live.

She approached the big Camden Road junction, where the juggernauts swung round from an arterial road into a city road too small for them. A pedestrian crossing was provided, and an occasional gap in the traffic organised for those on foot, those rash enough to want to cross from one side to another. In the middle of the road was a narrow island, with a Belisha beacon in the middle for the use of pedestrians caught there before the traffic flow started again. Step backwards, and northbound vehicles would mow you down: step forwards, and southbound ones would do it equally well.

Today Jason and Isabel were trapped on the island. In her hurry to get him to school she had miscalculated the time available to cross. She held his hand tightly. With them, squashing them, on the island was a woman with a perambulator, which she had to turn sideways for safety, and a man in a hat and a good suit. She noticed the hat, for hats were rare. The man saw what he thought was a gap, and darted forward to cross; changed his mind and leaped back for safety, knocking Isabel backwards into the road behind her. She let go Jason's hand, instinctively.

The lorry that bore down on her as she staggered back into the road braked, screeched, swerved. Drivers shouted abuse, blared horns. She was frightened but not hurt. The man with the hat lifted it and smiled at her. 'I'm sorry, ma'am.' The voice was American. The face was familiar. Black-eyed, swarthy, frightening Joe. He smiled, and this time darted off between the traffic with ease and safety. The woman with the pram turned humble, honest eyes upon her. She was Indian, in a sari, lost in a foreign, dangerous land where to step forward or back was to die. When the expected gap in the traffic occurred Isabel helped her across.

'Is that what they mean,' said Jason. 'A miss is as good as a mile?'

211

'I expect so,' said Isabel.

'What would happen to me if you died?'

'Daddy would look after you, or friends; there's always someone.'

'Okay,' said Jason, equably.

'Mrs Pelotti,' said Isabel, 'you won't let anyone other than Homer or me take him away, will you?'

'Of course not,' said Mrs Pelotti. 'The trouble with having celebrities in the school is we have to start worrying about kidnappings. As if custody snatchings weren't bad enough.'

'I'm not such a celebrity as all that,' said Isabel.

'Bad enough,' said Mrs Pelotti. 'And of course all mothers are celebrities to their children, and *vice versa*. In the middle classes, at any rate. Just try and collect him in time, Ms Rust. Your turn today, still?'

'Of course.'

'I thought you might have changed your minds. Since it's usually his father's delivery day, and here you are.'

'He had a puncture. The system doesn't work like that, Mrs Pelotti. I'll still be picking him up.'

'I'll try and remember.'

Little children worked industriously in ordered classrooms, and piped in gentle song. The lilt of recorders followed her out of school. No one followed her. Why should they? Everyone knew well enough where she would be going, and how impossible it would be for her not to be there. And perhaps, after all, it had not been Joe who had so nearly killed her. Easy enough, the circumstances being what they were, for her to imagine that any American would be Pete or Joe, and any untoward incident their doing.

She called Dr Gregory and left a message to say she would be there at five. She wished him to acknowledge her sanity; she wanted him to tell her what to do. A decision which involved only herself was easy enough to make; one which involved husband and child as well could only be difficult. It was an argument, she could see, against wifehood and motherhood: the endless balancing of goods and bads, happiness and unhappiness; pushing this one a little further up the seesaw of their lives, drawing that one a little back, so that the inevitable bumps and jags were rendered as smooth and painless as possible. Woman's work. This time, whatever she did, the jolt would be considerable; and they would be lucky to escape with their lives, for the play-ground itself had suddenly become dangerous – split by forces people had talked about for years but no one had really taken seriously.

'Tell Dr Gregory,' she said to Mrs Gregory, 'that just because there's a plot against you doesn't mean you can't imagine one as well.'
'Just a minute,' said Mrs Gregory, 'wait until I find a pencil.'
'Oh never mind,' said Isabel, and put down the phone.

32

Joe and Pete went to visit Elphick. They went first to the BBC TV Centre at Wood Lane, where they were refused admission by the security man at the gate. They wore good suits, and ties and polished shoes, but there was, by now, something in their demeanour which made honest men fearful. They had not started out with it: they had acquired it.

'You documentary men know some funny people,' said the security man, on the internal line, 'but these two will need a lot of vouching for before *I* let them in.'

'I'm Special Features,' said Elphick, 'as it happens. But I'll come down in person.'

'I'm not letting them through without body-searching them, sir. You'll have to explain that to them.'

It seemed simpler to Elphick to take them back to his apartment than to argue with the gateman.

'Say whatever you have to say and go,' he said to them, when they were there, settled, with white wine on the rocks in their hands, feet up — fortunately on the rickety chairs rather than on the velour couch from Harrods.

'Kindly say your lines and leave the stage.'

They said them. They looked round at the Braque and the onyx table and the alabaster lamp and congratulated him on his choice of resaleable items. They would not always be there to provide, they warned him.

'It's a long long time since I've wanted you to provide,' he said. 'These days the looming Communist Menace has somehow lost its sense of loom. The one great argument you have against it is that it puts its writers in prison. I've worked with a lot of writers since we all started out together, and my considered opinion is that a whole lot more of them ought to be put in prison.'

He laughed. It was half a joke. Pete and Joe looked immeasurably shocked.

'As for your sort of freedom,' he said, 'it only seems to amount to the right to shoot each other at random and at will.'

Pete and Joe, Kitten and Hot Potato, felt their firearms warm and bulky in their armpits. Elphick knew well enough that they were there. He seemed not to care.
'You took five thousand dollars from us three days ago, and came up with the goods,' remarked Pete.
'Of course I did,' said Elphick. 'Your interests and mine coincided. Why not? But what do you want now?'
'We don't want her going out live tonight.'
'What about next week, or the week after?'
'We'll look after that. You just see about tonight.'
'I don't want any harm coming to her,' said Elphick. 'TV is short of good people.'
'Of course not,' said Pete.

'We don't wage war on women,' said Joe.

'How much?' asked Elphick.

'Ten thousand,' said Pete.

'Dollars or pounds?'

'Pounds,' said Pete, after a little hesitation.

Elphick mused a little.

'We have some interesting intimate footage here of you and Ms Rust,' said Joe, losing patience.

'Do you, by Jove!' said Elphick. 'Wired, tapped, filmed and bugged. I might have known. I hope you enjoyed them.'

'Your wife might be interested,' said Joe.

'Ex-wife,' said Elphick.

'Your employers, then.' There was a pleading edge to Joe's voice.

'Book a viewing theatre,' said Elphick. 'I'll take the money at the door.'

Pete frowned Joe into silence.

'A man's got to work out what kind of society he wants his kids to live in,' said Pete, 'and fight to acquire it. He can't sit on the fence.'

'I can,' said Elphick. 'How much did you say?'

'Fifteen thousand pounds,' said Pete.

'It's not much,' said Elphick, 'with inflation running at fifteen per cent.' But he took it, as Pete peeled off the notes from his billfold.

Elphick showed them to the door.

'I wouldn't have let her go on anyway,' he said. 'She has a shocking black eye. It doesn't do to let the viewers know

their personalities are flesh and blood. And I have her best
interests at heart, as ever. But thank you, anyway.'

Pete and Joe looked at each other, once they were out on
the street.
'Bunch of European crazies,' said Pete. He was very angry.

33

Listen! It's peaceful in here, in the dark. Come in. Sear your eyes with a poker – join me! No, I mean it. It's worth it. The mercy of your fellow men will astound you brisk and wary sighted people – they will help you at the kerb, cut your meat for you. Men will offer you their sexual gifts; women will arrange your hair. They will see you first off sinking ships: give you priority of escape as the home for the disabled burns down. You cannot read but by God you can talk. You have very little choice of occupation, true, but comparatively few obligations. You will have no one to worry about except yourself.

And think of the sights you are spared. You hear the mother shriek at the child, but you don't have to see the blow; or the look on the child's face – need not witness the destruction of hope. You don't have to see the glance your lover gives another woman; the sneer of the waiter goes unobserved. You don't have to notice the new grey hair on your best friend's head; or the growing elephantiasis of your grandfather's leg. Travel escorted on the underground, and you will be spared the sight of junkies, weeping women, drunken men, whores, pimps, and wrappers of junk food, the sticky mess of vomit and urine, of soot piling into corners. You will not see the extent of the depression and the will to die that crowds our city streets.

You will live by courtesy of social workers – that is, amongst the middle class and their kindness. You are no threat to them. They can and will be kind. People are. My grandfather has lived eighty healthy years: his leg has been bad for only one of them. See it as an eight per cent misfortune: not a total one. The junkie was a pretty gentle lad. His end is not pretty, but his beginning was. It is not all bad, I promise you. I know. I learn little dancing ways around the great blazing beacons of misfortune that light all our lives. Because I cannot see, I cannot be blinded by the light. I find my way.

Of course I cannot see. I do not want to see. Do you?

34

'Isabel,' said Elphick, as she sat in the Make-up room, with hard lights turned upon her eye, to see how the thick tinted make-up that now covered cheek and brow would stand up to the viewer's inspection – 'you can't go on.'

'I have to,' said Isabel. 'Who else is there to do it?'

'Alice,' said Elphick, and Alice was led in, smiling and victorious, brimming with achievement and love, and the vindication of years of struggle and sacrifice.

'You don't mind, Isabel,' said Alice. 'It's only one pro-gramme, after all,' but Isabel knew she would presently be eased out altogether by Alice, or someone like her, and that her carnal liaison with Elphick would do her no good; on the contrary. She was now, in Elphick's eyes, on a par with Alice: flesh and blood, not a creature of mystery.

'It isn't really my black eye, is it?' she said to him in the box, for he required her presence at his elbow.

'It's a number of things,' he said. 'You're too clever for the programme and it shows: it's too down-market for you. It suits Alice, who's as stupid as the people she interviews.'

'Are you firing me?' she asked.

'Only in your own interests,' he said. 'I think you should

lie low for a little, and say as little as possible to anyone about anything.'

And he turned and smiled at her, in what she felt was genuine affection and concern.

'You can't save the world,' he said. 'You'd better just try saving yourself, the way I do.'

After that lights flashed, monitors hummed, earphones buzzed and they were too busy to say anything. Alice did wonderfully well, everyone agreed, and Isabel was obliged to stay later than usual for coffee and sandwiches afterwards, to show that she felt no animosity.

It was ten to four by the time she reached the White City underground platform. She would be late, again, collecting Jason from school. She considered calling Homer and asking him to do it, but realised that would save no time. She wondered if she should take a taxi, but the rush-hour traffic was gathering. To go by underground would be quicker. The train came into the station. She boarded it. She would have to change trains at Tottenham Court Road, on to the Northern line, to reach Camden Town. It occurred to her that she might be being followed, but also that there was an indignity in looking back. Nevertheless, she did so, once, and saw nothing remarkable, only the usual grey throng of commuters, black and white mixed, every colour of costume combined, as on a child's paint palette, to neutral muddiness. The very anonymity of what she saw frightened her: there was no protection in the world. The whole was composed of so many parts, that the loss of one of those parts would scarcely be noticed. She did not look round again.

Her legs and arms moved as if they were nothing to do with her. The extraordinary nature of recent events had drained those events of reality. She had always imagined that when in physical danger she would develop an acuteness of response and perception. Instead, she seemed to be partly anaesthetised; as a fly must be, just before the spider eats it. She felt, in fact, stupid, obtuse and lethargic: a not very good audience for her own life, unsure of when to applaud and when not to, when to laugh or when to cry, longing mostly just to go home.

She spoke aloud, and listened to what she was saying.

> 'Like one, that on a lonesome road
> Doth walk in fear and dread,
> And having once turned round walks on,
> And turns no more his head;
> Because he knows, a frightful fiend
> Doth close behind him tread.

Coleridge,' she told them. 'The Ancient Mariner.'
A little pool of space cleared around her, as commuters avoided contamination from the loony. It made her feel safer.

She stood on Platform Four. It was crowded. She stayed as far back as she could, but more and more people flowed in from the sides and eddies of movement caught her up and propelled her to the platform's edge. She wondered now, more than ever, why so few people died from falling on the rail, inadvertently toppled or deliberately pushed.

222

Even as she wondered, she felt strong hands in the small of her back, well centred and determined, and they pushed, and as the top half of her went forward, a foot — someone else's, surely, curled round her ankle and yanked it back. She began to topple: a train was coming: she could hear it: it roared and rumbled: it must almost be upon her: 'What about Jason,' she thought, indignantly, as if the mothers of small children were simply not allowed to die, and then she was moving backwards, upward, a hand of extraordinary strength grabbing first shoulder, then arm, and there she was, upright, on the platform, the train sliding in three uncomfortable inches from her nose, and the hand was relaxing.

It was a bony, withered hand, sprinkled with brown liver spots. An elderly woman, craggy-nosed, stared her in the eye. She seemed astonished and frightened and proud, all at once.

'But I just pulled you back,' said the woman. 'Someone pushed you — you fell — and I caught you. I never used to be strong.'
'It's adrenalin,' explained Isabel. 'I once saw a woman pick up a car which had a child pinned under it. She just picked it up, and moved it. But thank you very much,' she added, fearing to sound ungrateful. But the woman clearly found the event too remarkable and too embarrassing to discuss further, and melted back into the crowd. And whoever had pushed would be far away, by now.

Isabel's calmness seemed to disconcert the little cluster of people who had witnessed the incident. I suppose I should scream, or shout, she thought, but all I want to do is to get back to ordinariness, to pretend nothing out of the way has happened. The train doors opened. Everyone got on. The incident was over.

Isabel, who had woken that morning believing that life stretched ahead, endlessly, could now see such a view was hopelessly optimistic. You had to be grateful for the next ten minutes.

I should tell the police, she told herself. That's what people do. The police will believe me. They know that things like this happen all the time. Homer won't like it, but I'll have to do it. When I've collected Jason I'll go round to the police station. I'll leave him with Jennifer. She'll guard him with her life. How do people know so much about me? Who's telling? Perhaps it's Mrs Pelotti?

But that was madness. Because danger threatened from one direction, you could not see it all around. She felt Dr Gregory's shrewd wandering eye upon her and her fear subsided. She wanted her mother. She wanted the dusty boredom of the yellow horizons, the flat, hot landscape.

She was fifteen minutes late at the school. The building was quiet and echoey, as if it slept. She felt an intruder. She went straight to Mrs Pelotti's room, where there was a light burning and where she knew she would find Jason. She did not dare think otherwise.

Mrs Pelotti worked under a neon desk light, writing. 'It's you, Ms Rust,' she said, unsurprised. 'Still wandering, looking for the lost soul of your child. I'm doing secondary-school selections this week, or I wouldn't be here at all, and you'd be a sort of ghost.'

'Where's Jason?'

'Jason? Your husband collected him. Just as well, you being so late. Sherry? You look very pale.'

'No, thank you. Homer collected Jason?'

'Yes.'

'But it's Thursday.'

'He must have known you'd be late. Perhaps he knew you'd be delayed.'

'Yes,' said Isabel, patterns fitting, interlocking. 'I expect that's what he thought.'

The sense of being a spectator at her own life intensified.

Homer. A spy, existing only to observe, report and mould events if and when he could. Did that mean he didn't love her, never had? Of course. Homer, playing games, all words and kisses and adopted attitudes. Easy enough. Could you live with someone for six years and not know the person you were married to?

Of course. It happened all the time. Women married to rapists, bigamists, con men, adulterers are all when it comes to it taken by surprise. No, your honour, I had no idea. He had blood on his hands but he said he'd been killing a rabbit: eye make-up on his vest but he said it was ink from a leaking pen. I believed him. Marriage was a breeding ground for deception. No one expected it. You'd think in bed – well, of course, in retrospect. Homer's efficiency which only lately she had construed as coldness: the sense of no new discovery, ever. Well, he knew it all already, didn't he.

Homer, sent in by Joe and Pete on a watching brief. She'd never escaped. Once with Dandy, always with Dandy, if only by proxy. Of course you didn't meet men on aircraft, when in flight from one life, and start another. It was the old life continuing. Prince Charming was a fictional creation.

Her flight from Dandy had not been action, it had been reaction. Pete and Joe knew well enough how to frighten her, how to time her departure. They, no doubt, had stuffed dollar bills in Dandy's wallet to get her back to Heathrow. Homer was waiting for her there. She did not think Dandy had been too much involved: he had his dignity: he would just have asked her to go.

She should be grateful that they had not simply disposed of her, killed her, but had invested so much energy and time and money in a polite attempt to keep her alive.

Had she not given birth to Jason, who carried Dandy's genes, been the mother of the would-be President's child, they would scarcely, she imagined, have gone to such lengths for so long. Or perhaps Dandy was part of it, and thought of her with enough affection to wish to preserve her.

Homer worshipped Jason as Dandy's son, not his own. His concern for her, Isabel, had always been as Jason's mother. That, in retrospect, was clear enough.

'Can I give you a lift somewhere?' asked Mrs Pelotti.
She was on her feet, holding Isabel's arm. Isabel found comfort in it.

'Look,' she said. 'Jason may not be in for a little. I have to organise a few things.'

'Well yes,' said Mrs Pelotti, 'until the election's over, perhaps you had. I've heard talk; everyone had dismissed it as nonsense until *Cosmopolitan* came out. Like father, like son. Jason has such a strong personality. He's not easy, you know, but we do our best. I look forward to quite an influx of middle-class parents next term, one way and another. Don't worry about Jason, if he's with your husband. He'll look after him. He's very fond of him, genuinely. I can tell, you know.'

'I believe you can,' said Isabel. It was some sort of comfort: a small glow of certainty in tumultuous black: a wave from the stage at curtain call, in forgiveness and reassurance.

She would go to Dr Gregory, lie on his couch, sort things out. She was stunned, shocked and afraid. She was also right. She wanted to tell him that. 'If I didn't tell my husband,' she would say, 'it was because he wasn't loveable. I registered him as a stranger because that is what he was. You were wrong and I was right.'

She took a taxi to Harley Street. No one bumped into her or pushed her. The fare clocked up in an orderly way.

The taxi driver was morose. If her life was in crisis, if she lived only by the skin of her teeth, if what she had believed in and lived by – her marriage to Homer – had vanished between one hour and the next, what was it to him? She was a fare, not a person. As he, to her, was driver, not human being. There was a justice in it. For all she knew he had just come back from hospital with a verdict of terminal cancer.

'You all right, mate?' he asked, when he took her fare, proving her wrong, and himself concerned.

'Do I not look all right?'

'No.'

'I just had some bad news.'

'What, on the marital front?'

'That's right.'

'The answer is,' he said, 'never to get married,' and while she pondered this, in her new, slow way, he drove off into the gloom without handing over her change.

The lifts in Dr Gregory's office block were crowded going down, almost empty going up. She wondered why it seemed so important to her that Dr Gregory should know that she'd been right about Homer, and he'd been wrong. Because, she supposed, the areas in which she'd been successful, or even sensible, had narrowed so suddenly. She needed at least this one area of self-respect if she was to survive the next days, the next weeks. And for once, surely, he would abandon his principle of non-intervention and tell her what to do. Puppets had to have strings to pull them, or they just lay lifeless.

She was glad she was so numb. Presently, no doubt it would begin to hurt.

Dr Gregory's receptionist had gone home. The hat stand was empty, the typewriter covered. Dr Gregory's door was ajar: the light was on, the gentle sound of afternoon music came through the air. She felt safe – as if she was a child and here was the father she had never had: the source of wisdom, power and kindness. What would Dr Gregory make of that? She laughed aloud. A clear and resounding case of positive transference. Well, he would wean her away, no doubt, but little by little, and kindly.

She didn't love Homer. That was the great, the wonderful discovery. She had not wanted him to leave her in the ordinary way, but for him to snap out of existence, for Homer never to have been, as it were, was not undilutedly grievous. She was affronted and appalled and humiliated to discover his treachery: she was distressed not just for herself but for all her friends and colleagues and fans and sympathisers, that this rare and wonderful marriage of hers and Homer's, this match of equals, this coming together of male and female on level terms, should have proved a sham: worse than a sham, a calculated mockery.

'Dr Gregory,' she would say, 'I used to have a terrible dream when I was about ten. I would be in some public place and all of a sudden my knickers would fall around my ankles and all my friends would turn and laugh. I remember what you call the feeling-tone of the dream so well – it is what I feel now. A humiliation so profound I would rather die than go on living.'

She must have moaned a little. She heard Dr Gregory's voice from the inner office.

'Isabel, is that you? Laughing and moaning out there in the dark? I think you should come in and tell me all about it, and not keep it to yourself.'

Isabel went in to his office: out of pooled darkness into the warm light. She thought perhaps he used pink light bulbs in his surgery, and not the usual opal pearl. He sat at his desk, writing.

'Lie down,' he said. 'I won't be a moment.'

Isabel lay down. Presently she heard the faint clatter as he laid down his pen.
'Carry on,' he said.

'Two people tried to murder me today,' said Isabel, 'to get me out of the way. There's a spy somewhere in my life. I'm pretty sure it's Homer. He knew I wouldn't be collecting Jason, he thought I wouldn't be able to because I'd be dead.'

There was silence from Dr Gregory.

'Worse things happen at sea,' said Isabel, brightly. It was a phrase her mother used a lot when she was young. The child Isabel, who never saw the sea at all until she was seventeen, was prepared to believe her. Worse things happened at sea. Horses kicked you on land; sharks took off whole limbs, sometimes chumped you up altogether. Only of course you could always stay out of the sea or just paddle. Difficult to stay out of the way of horses, when you had to cross their paddock to get to your own front door and your mother said you should pat their rumps as you passed, to show there was no ill feeling. She realised that a sick feeling she had was to do with Jason.
'It's just Jason,' she said. 'Where's Jason? What am I going to do?'

She found she was crying. Still Dr Gregory said nothing. There was a kind of shuffling noise behind her.

'Jason's okay, Isabel,' said Homer. 'He's being looked after. We just need a talk, you and I.'

She sat up. Homer and Dr Gregory were standing companionably by the window.

'Defenestration,' she said. 'Death by falling out of a window.'

'No, no,' said Homer. 'Too untidy, and instantly suspect. And Isabel, I have too much respect for you to try and force you to your death. So I am sure has Dr Gregory. Pete and Joe, your American friends from way back, are clumsy and desperate and extremely stupid and I have tried to stand between them and you.'

'Thank you, Homer,' said Isabel.

'Worse,' he said, 'they have been ineffective, and time is running out.'

'Do you do this kind of thing for the money, Dr Gregory?' asked Isabel. She moved over to the desk and sat on it and swung her legs and rather admired her insouciance.

'Everyone works for money,' said Dr Gregory. 'Even psychoanalysts. But principle comes first.'

'Did you make it up, Homer?' asked Isabel. 'Did you make it up, about Jason biting and wetting the bed? Because now I come to think of it I never actually saw any of it. Except once, when Jason bit Bobby. And then some marks on your ankle you could have made yourself. I just took your word.'

'I wanted to get you to Dr Gregory,' said Homer.

'You have deceived me, Homer,' said Isabel, plaintively.

A little voice, in the face of enormous wrong. The casting director had got it wrong. This was not a part which called for insouciance. She would try it another way.

'Isabel,' said Homer patiently, 'if you recall it was you who

231

deceived me. You pretended Jason was mine and married me under false pretences. In a better age, in the one we hope to bring about, that would of course legally invalidate the marriage. As it is, and always has been, the marriage is morally invalid.'

Isabel opened and then closed her mouth. She thought that if the emergency stopped and she could inhabit her body again, that she would have a bad headache. The right side of her face felt sticky. She wiped away remnants of pan-stick from around her eye. There seemed little hope that she was in a play: that all of a sudden applause would break out and she'd find she'd got it right. She remembered the vividness of a dream she'd once had, when all her teeth had fallen out. Waking to find it not true, she had cried for joy. There was to be no waking now. Perhaps the only escape was in a profounder sleep.

'Where's Jason?' she demanded, 'what have you done with Jason?' She felt mean-eyed and nasty. Waves of alternate feeling passed over her, hot and cold, and unhealthily like fever. She liked the meanness, the irritation; it was hopeful. If she treated Homer badly, pettily, he might somehow return to being what he had been. Homer, despised. Oh yes, she thought, despised. Ever so slightly despised. Homo washing-upticus.

'Jason's having a milk shake down below,' said Homer. 'You can see him from here.'

Isabel moved over to the window and looked down, and there, where the Georgian façade of the road opposite gave way to a low concrete shopping arcade, sat Jason, her son, at a table in the window of a milk bar, bright new American style. He was flanked by two men. All drank milk shakes through straws.

'Pete and Joe,' said Isabel. Feeling was beginning to return, that was it, like pain to a tooth when the dentist's injection wears off. Real life, real pain.

'Overpaid, overarmed and over here,' said Homer. 'What I was hoping to avoid. They'll look after Jason. For the time being. He is the President's son.'

'Dandy may not be President,' said Isabel, sharply, 'and he won't be if I have anything to do with it.'

If you could be killed it made you real enough to kill. If they wanted to kill you, you must be dangerous. That was the secret she'd been waiting for.

Her Australian accent was back: she noticed it. She was down to the origins of her being. Flakes of good behaviour peeled away, like layers from a stale chocolate bar, held together by its wrapper.

'Homer,' observed Dr Gregory, 'there we have the root of the trouble. She will never fully come to terms with her anger with her father. She misplaces it into aggression against the world and the whole male sex. If I'd had more time with her this might possibly have been avoided. But she kept missing appointments. Patients are their own worst enemy.'

Homer seemed not to be listening. He smiled quite kindly at Isabel and patted the couch, so she sat down again, docilely. He sat beside her.

'Isabel, I want to appeal to your better nature. It is there, somewhere, beneath your sloppy liberalism, your hysteria, and your female irrationality. If you co-operate with me I can save Jason. I can take him back home, leave him for my parents to raise. He'll get a decent haircut, a proper education; early nights. He'll be safe, he'll have standards; he'll grow up into a good man. He needs discipline, Isabel. Boys do. He can be anonymous. I'll see to that.'

'What do you mean by "co-operate"? Keep silent? Lose Jason? You're joking, Homer.'

'She won't keep to it,' warned Dr Gregory. 'Sooner or later she'll decide her mission is to save the world, in the sacred name of Woman. Heredity probably plays quite a part here. She may not be unlike her father in her psychological make-up. He abandoned wife and child on political grounds. Which is psychic murder, of course, when you consider the wrecks that are left behind. I see them all the time. I hope Ivel manages to bring in the strong family law he promises. Too late for this generation: the next one will benefit.'

He spoke to thin air. Homer looked only at Isabel. He laid his hand on hers. She felt a pang of simple sexual desire for him, more startling and severe than any she had felt during her marriage to him.

He shook his head at her. He seemed to know what she was thinking and feeling. Presumably he had paid more attention to what went on in her head than she had in his. It was his profession, after all.

'Homer,' said Isabel. 'Did you like any of it? The furniture, the house, the neighbours, the theatre, the books, anything?'

'Not really,' said Homer. 'I tried to acquire a taste for it all, but it never really fitted.'

'Jogging?'

'Oh yes. I liked that.'

'Did you like me?'

'Sometimes. On and off. Of course. You were often charming. I didn't like your ideas. I didn't like the way you were bringing up Jason. Jason! What a name. You were very obstinate. But yes, I liked you. On and off.'

'Our friends?'

'For the most part they seemed stupid, and ignorant. The men weak and the women ugly, and making themselves uglier day by day with every fashionable new opinion they picked up. I don't blame you so much, Isabel. You are the product of a sick society: a broken home, poor moral education. The tragedy is, you need not be the way you are. With God's help, in future, women like you will do what they can to help society, not destroy it.'

'God?' enquired Isabel. 'I suppose you prayed, after I'd gone to sleep?'

'Yes,' said Homer. 'I am not like you. I do not put my trust in my fellow men; I put it in God.' His hand still lay on her arm, a moral rather than a physical restraint.

'It was interesting. I learned a lot. You were smart enough, but you had a veil over your eyes. Where I saw misery and degradation and confusion, you saw something to be sought after, to be worked for. You were happy enough for Jason to be brought up in the gutter. That I found hard to forgive.'

'Mrs Pelotti's school? The gutter?'

'She's a good woman; she tries hard. But the idealogues have too firm a grasp on education — they've infiltrated. It's past curing. Of course there are riots in the streets; a total breakdown of discipline. It's what they wanted, what they've achieved. Apart from anything else, Isabel, Jason is Dandy's son: he deserves better than that. He has to be rescued from Mrs Pelotti and the meanness of the city streets.'

'And while I'm alive,' said Isabel.
'Exactly,' said Homer.
'Ah,' said Isabel. All became abundantly clear. She was not to be allowed to live, because she was a source of danger, moral and physical, to her son. Perhaps all fathers felt like this, in their hearts? That the mother damaged the male child, sapped his strength, warped his sexuality? Perhaps they were right: perhaps the piercing love she felt for Jason was indeed unhealthy. But that was nonsense. These two men, who between them claimed to know her heart, knew nothing. The world, left to itself, was an easy, natural place: ending her ordinary affection for her son would cure little, and achieve less. It would certainly make him miserable. She'd known a woman who'd committed suicide and killed her five-year-old daughter at the same time. How wicked some said: those were the more educated. How brave, others said, less sophisticated. The child is the mother's property: if she goes, she must take the child with her.

Jason was six; he had his own life, his own identity. The umbilical cord was stretched to breaking point, ready to snap. A month ago she would have said no, he cannot survive without me. If I go, he goes. But in so short a time, things had altered. Jason used her like a servant, he loved her, but he could do without her, if he had to. If he was dead, she would not want to live: she would be too wounded, too much a part of her existence gone to survive,

236

even if she wanted. There was, when it came to it, no choice.

Her two watchers, minders of her mind, but not her soul, thought they bullied her and confused her, but she saw through their tricks, and oddly enough, came to the same conclusion. She must die, and Jason must live.

'I suppose,' said Isabel, 'you just want me to walk down there into the street and consent to be killed?'
'Yes,' said Homer.
'In front of Jason?'
'That wouldn't be a good idea,' said Dr Gregory. 'We don't want the boy traumatised.'
'I'm not a fool,' said Homer, crossly. 'And I have the child's best interests at heart.'
'For example,' said Isabel, 'that he should grow up motherless?'

Homer seemed embarrassed.

'It is better,' he said, 'than that he shouldn't grow up at all.'
'That's the alternative?' asked Isabel.
'You must see that it is,' said Homer. 'You can't be relied upon to live anonymously. We can't go on together. Nor am I in a position to control Pete and Joe and their friends, however much I would like to. All I can retrieve from the situation is Jason, at any rate for the time being, and that, if you will co-operate. If the rumours which already exist about Jason gain credence by any suspicion or doubt as to the cause of your death, then I will not be able to help your child. These are desperate times we live in, and the

lives of one woman and one child do not weigh very heavily in the balances of power. I don't expect you to understand: you are a woman, and emotive. Women do not have the same capacity for self-sacrifice as men do; or only in relation to their children, and that is a matter of instinct.'

'Quite true,' said Isabel, 'there weren't many women in the Light Brigade. Theirs not to reason why, theirs but to do and die. Can I have time to think about this?'

'No. There is nothing to think about. Besides, you have a capacity for instant decision. Everyone applauds it.'

Isabel removed her arm from the control of the grudging, murderous, envious stranger who sat beside her.

'Were you jealous?' she asked. 'Is that it? Because I lived a public life, and was a woman?'

'No,' he said, and laughed, and that was familiar: a short derisive laugh. 'The male-female struggle never really was an issue, Isabel. Window dressing: a sponge for radical energy. And how could you think I would be interested in the applause of fools, or the earnest discussions of idiots? Consensus achieves nothing. Real power, real influence, is a secret thing. You never did have power, Isabel. How could you? You opened your mouth and said what you thought, which was only ever what you felt.'

'Like Dandy.'

'All too much like Dandy. But it's too late to go back there, either.'

'And you seriously think I will go out there and die? Do you mean to shoot me? Or run me over, or what?'

'All I want you to do is look right instead of left and step into the traffic. It will be very quick.'

'I don't think I could,' said Isabel. 'Even if I decided to.'

'You have decided to,' said Homer, 'and you will.' His

238

voice was steady and almost kind. There was no trace of madness or excitability in it.

'Couldn't Dandy help me, somehow?'

'No,' said Homer, and Isabel believed him.

'It's very interesting about you and Dandy,' said Homer. 'You succumbed to something there: you contracted a terminal illness.'

'Love,' said Isabel.

'Perhaps,' he conceded, and Dr Gregory, opening his mouth no doubt to say something or other about neurotic need, closed it again. The greater word seemed to suit the greater occasion.

'It is a far, far better thing, etcetera, etcetera,' said Isabel to Homer. 'I hope you will allow me some nobility of soul.' She continued, she discovered, to want his good opinion – as wives running from dreadful marriages will continue to want their husbands' permission to leave long after they have gone.

'Of course I will,' said Homer. 'And I hope Jason inherits it.'

Isabel went to the window and looked briefly down at Jason. Nothing, she thought, will ever be exactly right for the child; he was misbegotten. Perhaps he would contrive a little better than she had done, and bring his own children safely into the world. It was, she supposed, all one generation could hope to do for the rest. Sooner or later mothers died. That was natural. The death of children struck a blow forward into time, and was terrible. But she could not rear the President's child, if the President did not wish it. The weight of power was too much for her to bear. She could not live harried and observed: there was nowhere for her to hide – no means, in the face of such savage male disapproval, whereby she could earn her living or live in anonymity. The power of the Press, seen as the common man's defence against the force of princes and beings, worked in her disfavour. They would seek her out as once, in her careless past, she had sought out the innocent victims of random events and flung them, shrinking and blinded, into the spotlight. She could not even cry, 'I didn't know. I didn't understand.' She did. She had. She had said to herself giving birth to Jason, 'This will be difficult; dangerous,' never quite believing that what she said was true – that some magic was not available to save her, alone amongst women, from the consequences of her actions. There was not. Weights and balances. Give and take. This hand gains, that hand loses. Jason lives, plucked by her out of the fringy edges of disaster, given life. Isabel dies. Without the father, the President, there was not enough life to go round.

She looked into her future, as it might have been, and saw all the things she was to be spared. She was not to have to grow old, and be despised and pitied. She was not to have to suffer the body's dereliction and decay. She was not to have to live through the death of friends, one by one: see the emptiness of ambition, the folly of worldly achievement. She was not to have to suffer more deceit, more humiliation at the hands of other Homers. She would not be betrayed, again, by the likes of Dandy. More powerfully still, she was not to have to see Jason grow out of his present perfection – all hope, all promise – into flawed and ordinary adulthood. She looked at the world, in fact, with a suicide's eye. She had to.

'I don't want Jason watching,' she repeated. 'I want my death theoretical: a matter of my not being there, rather than anything else. The same for him as it will be for me. The party one was obliged to miss.'

If you went willingly to your death, it seemed to Isabel, you finally acknowledged that other people existed. That their reality was as true as yours, and you had not, after all, made them all up in your head. At the party you missed, people fell in love and out of it, and lives were changed and destinies mapped out, just the same as if you'd been there.

Homer drew her to the window. His touch excited her, now that he was the Angel of Death, not the slave of life. 'Look down there,' he said.

Downstairs in the café Jason now sat with his back to the window. Pete and Joe faced out into the street.

'Very well,' said Isabel. 'But I don't want him seeing my body. One brings children so gradually to the concept of death, I don't want all that good work undone.'

Dr Gregory turned on the radio.
'Is that to drown my screams?' asked Isabel, a remark she at once regretted, since it seemed to be in bad taste.
'We listen to the news,' said Homer, rather stiffly. 'They carry quite a bit on the US election.'

He opened the door for Isabel.

'Don't go by lift,' he said. 'Go down by the stairs.'

He smiled at Isabel in a friendly fashion. I have been such a small part of his life, she thought, and he has played so large a part in mine. He engaged reason, and I engaged feeling.

There were thirty steps down to the lobby. Isabel stood at the top and counted them. One for every year of her life.

She thought she should feel fear, but she did not. She felt her pulse: it beat steadily: a little fast, not much.

Twelve steps down. My life in Europe, gone: a life that included a dozen lovers; a child, however misbegotten, a husband, however misconstrued. False life.

She hesitated, mutinous. Why is it accepted, why do I accept that the child's life comes before the mother's? That the new fresh shoot is more valuable than the cracked and crabby branch. I could have six more children. If they existed, already, I would not so willingly face extinction. My responsibility to them could outweigh my duty to Jason.

Another eight steps down and she was fifteen, and the last thing she meant to do was die.

She sat down upon the step. She thought of Jason: his small limbs, his lambent eyes, his slow smiles; the prescience of male maturity.

If he was a girl, she thought, I would not do this. I would be more practical, less reverent. I would see a daughter as an offshoot of me. I would be less prepared to sacrifice myself.

Five steps further down. The last steps, the last breaths. What was existence, anyway? Consciousness?

Someone called aloud, 'Mummy!' and she knew it was herself. Other children called their mothers mum, or ma; it was left to children of tender English descent to say 'Mummy'.

Was this where so much sacrifice, so much dedication, led?

There was a kind of glory in it. A few more steps, and she was in the lobby, and confused. She had never quite expected to get so far.

Now what?

Would they send a lorry, or did she have to choose one? How could she know she'd die quickly; or trust them to be competent. It seemed they could not even kill her without her help. She assumed they'd have ways of seeing to it. If not on the road, in the ambulance, in the hospital thereafter.

The porter at the entrance smiled. She smiled and nodded back. Co-operate. She must be seen to die happily.

Jason had his back to her. They had moved his chair so he need not see whatever was to be seen. She was glad of that.

She stood at the edge of the kerb, momentarily, looking carefully to the left, while a wall of traffic advanced towards her from the right.

She saw Jason waving at her from the other side of the road. His face was tearful. He was shouting at her. She could not hear what he was saying: she was frightened that he would ignore the traffic and run across to her. So many children were killed, chasing balls or seeing friends, forgetting caution in a flurry of excitement. But Jason was well trained. He hopped up and down on the kerb.

'Careful, lady,' said the porter, holding her back until the traffic was past. 'Now you can go,' and he pushed her across. She reached the other side without incident. Jason ran up to her, buried his head in her dress, tearful and resentful.

'I can't pay. They went away without paying. I haven't any money.'

She took him back into the cafe. Pete and Joe were gone. She ordered him another milk shake.

'That's three,' said the waitress reproachfully. She had black hair streaked with green, and a pale face. 'I was going to call the police. I didn't know what those men were doing with a nice little boy like that. Then you came along.'

'They're friends of his father's,' said Isabel, 'that's all.'

The waitress raised her eyebrows as if to say 'fine father'. 'Why did they go?' asked Isabel, of Jason.

'They just got up and walked out,' said Jason. 'They seemed cross about something. I don't think it was me.'

'Isn't it awful about Dandy Ivel,' said the waitress, bringing Isabel her coffee.

'What about him?'

'He's dead,' said the waitress. 'Stroke. He always was rather pink, I thought, but it might have been the colour on my telly. Still, he was young for it. Poor man. Perhaps he was on drugs. They all are over there, aren't they? Think of Elvis Presley.'

'Is that why the men went, do you think?' asked Isabel. 'Because they heard the news on the radio?'

'Might well be,' said the waitress. 'That's what I thought. They looked at each other and they just got up and went, leaving the little boy in a terrible state. I don't think you should let them take him out. Of course, it's nothing to do with me.'

'I'd better have some coffee,' said Isabel. She was shivering: but she was real. Her nail varnish was chipped. Presently she'd see to that. She, who had nearly been nothing, was now something again.

Homer and Dr Gregory left the building opposite and walked away, quietly and calmly. Joe and Pete fell in behind. They turned the corner, disappeared, passed out of her life. She did not think she would see any of them again. They would have other things to do, new kings to make: the old world to save in a different way. Dandy would never come to power. Jason was saved. A fatherless child, like so many others.

Poor Dandy! Dead. Memories shrivelled inside her, turned to ashes, meaningless. Only Jason, ever, had been real.

She took Jason to the cinema to see Buck Rogers. Jason

referred to the cinema as 'the big telly'. Isabel seemed to remember thinking of television as the small cinema. So the world changes, she thought. She slept through most of the film; a dead, necessary, solid sleep.

When she got back to Wincaster Row Homer had gone, packed, taking with him his more formal clothes, and his jogging shoes.

He had taken in a small parcel from the postman, in his brief time back in the house, and left it on the hall table. It was for Jason, from her mother. She had sent it by express post. It was a small koala bear, in real fur. There was a note enclosed, for Isabel. 'It's time the little boy remembered his origins,' her mother wrote. 'Why don't you bring him over, for a holiday? I can help with the fare if that's what's stopping you. I sold the house for a good price: they say it's of historic interest. I'm living in Sydney now, with a view over the harbour.'

Isabel went round to see Maia.

'I'm selling the house,' she said. 'I'm going back home to see my mother. But there's a story I want to tell you, first, so you can hand it on.'

35

Isabel and Jason are safe. They live, to fight another day. Dandy it was who died, killed by the pills which were meant to save him. Jason lives on, in his father's image up and down, back and forth, pondering the nature of existence, ordering his mother about, under the brilliant Australian sky. His little foot kicks up the hot yellow sand: no longer scuffs the carpets of Wincaster Row. Perhaps he will belong to a new generation of man, who can find power enough inside themselves, and not go seeking for it in the exploitation and pillaging of women and the world; who can find their kingdom in inner and not outer space.

As for the others, I turn my face skywards, up towards the incandescence of the summit of my mountain of truth, but even that brilliance can hardly penetrate my blackness. I catch a glimmer here and there. Pete and Joe work for what is known as Organised Crime; and are more at ease within a simpler framework of loyalties and beliefs. He who is richest is best and what is good for profit is good for America, and *vice versa*. Pete's wife eventually ran off with Homer, whom she'd known from way back. Both had changed, within the decade. The habits of culture and kindness are catching – it is one of the few hopes we have. New ideas drop like lemon juice into icing sugar, and behold, everything changes, and is better.

Vera of course is dead and gone, before her time. She lies in an unmarked grave in an unknown place. Her little sister Marielle, frightened by Vera's sudden and unexplained disappearance, left Smoky Al and went back home, and presently married a businessman from Amsterdam, by whom she had girl twins, as if to make up as quickly as possible for her lost sister.

In the end, I think, looking out over Wincaster Row, at the green lawns where the rubble used to be, and where the children are now out playing, for the Sunday rain has stopped, and the day begins to borrow the energy of the coming week, virtue will triumph. Fate conspires to see that it does. Sunlight glances through the fuchsia hedge, making tiny, busy, moving patterns on mowed lawns. Jennifer, Hope, Hilary and Oliver have gone back to their ordinary lives – if any life can be considered ordinary.

Then I think, no, the struggle is eternal, and dreadful. There will never be peace. There is no pure and perfect victory for Good. Enough that misery, distress, nightmare and cruelty existed, to spoil for all eternity, backward and forward in time, the calm and unmoved face of God. Even should such things be wiped from our comprehension, once they were: and if they were, cannot be forgiven. This place where we live is hell: more, the game is never-ending. It is fire, torment, everlasting, as the Bible promised. I do not have the strength for it: nor do I believe I will simply be allowed to die, wink out. No such luck.

Sunlight glances through the fuchsia hedge, the sound of the bees retreats. It seems to me that there is something wrong with my hearing. Then I realise, no, how extraordinary: I am seeing – hearing diminished because sight has returned. I am cured. I was seized, just now, with such a fit of despair that I healed myself. I lost all hope and gained my sight. They did, after all, tell me I could, if I would. But they did not tell me the way to bring it about. They didn't know. How could they?

I run up and down the stairs. I laugh. I cry. Colours seem strange and mad and ever-changing. Print dances up and down before me, redolent of meaning, but not yet, not yet. I call Laurence: he sounds shocked, delighted, disappointed all at once. Hilary is more gaunt than I remembered, Hope prettier, Jennifer puffier and paler. In my mind they had drifted all together, become one. Woman. It isn't so. Now they spring apart into different beings. I call Helen at the delicatessen, she of the guilt and the grief and the potato salad in little bowed boxes, and she is silent, struck dumb as I was struck by sight. I speak to my mother: 'Mother. I am whole. I, your child, who was spoiled is whole again!' I call the hospital, the doctors, the specialists. Bells ring, brakes squeal, Laurence finds the number of the driver whose car hit me; phones him, releases him from the guilt he need never have felt. He weeps. Everyone seems pleased and gratified on my account. Smiles! I had forgotten smiles – they make so little noise.

What did it, they say? What caused it? A blow? A shock? A joke? How can I tell them the truth? God laughs at me, buffeting me around his universe. It is His peculiar pleasure.

Fay Weldon

Auto da Fay

A memoir

'You can't put this terrific book down.' *Daily Mail*

'It is an astonishing, gripping story, lightly and deftly told, without self-pity. It will delight her many fans.'
LYNN BARBER, *Daily Telegraph*

Fay Weldon, one of the pre-eminent writers of our times, has crammed more than most into her years. From the 1930s to the 2000s, Weldon has seen and lived it all. As a child in New Zealand, as young and poor in London, as unmarried mother, as wife, lover, novelist, feminist, anti-feminist, there are few waterfronts that she hasn't covered, few battles she hasn't fought.

'Effervescently funny, honest and insightful. Transports us across years of sadness, brightness, chaos, triumph. An exuberant and thoughtful treat.' ANDREA ASHWORTH.

'Wonderfully fluent and entertaining, revealing a life crammed with more gritty drama than a tea-time soap. You can always trust Fay to be provocative – and this time she excels herself.' VAL HENNESSY, *Daily Mail*

FLAMINGO

Fay Weldon

Puffball

A novel of urban deceit and rural passion

'Gripping'   *Observer*

Richard and Liffey haven't been married long. They are still madly in love, and in lust, and so, when Liffey suggests moving out of London to a country cottage in the middle of Somerset, Richard puts aside his reservations; he wants his young, pretty wife to be happy, after all.

But then the real world intervenes, and Richard must remain in London during the week and see his Liffey, now pregnant, only on weekends. And so that leaves poor Liffey, pregnant and alone, burdened, confused and frustrated by biological impulses which are suddenly overwhelming her. Can she rely on Mabs, her seemingly kindly neighbour, and Tucker, her rather over-friendly husband, for solace? Surely there can't be anything sinister in their motives – can there? At least she has no reason to doubt Richard's love for her – or does she?

With wit, wisdom, and a little dose of witchery, Fay Weldon reveals the conflicts that arise from the eternal struggle between male and female.

'Magical – she lays out the ingredients of her brew with a kind of manipulative glee, coolly moulding her characters and then neatly skewering them with mockery.'   *Daily Mail*

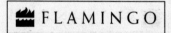 FLAMINGO

Fay Weldon

Nothing to Wear and Nowhere to Hide

'Short stories that slam doors. Funny, gossipy, quirky, explosive.'
Daily Telegraph

'These stories are the offspring of Angela Carter, darts barbed and stabbed in the throat of revenge. Weldon merges a quintessential, zappy Sixties sharpness with the ability to update her feel for the pulse of whatever is hip or chic or symbolic of each dawning era. She should be cloned.'
Scotsman

A spiky, feisty, hilarious collection of stories that expose women's clumsy, often doomed attempts to negotiate a smooth path through life. Bold, glamorous, sexy, unrepentant, Fay Weldon's heroines enthral and delight.

'Short and bittersweet. In true Weldon style we are presented with cynical musings on the roles forced on to – and in turn subverted by – modern womankind. Intelligent, tongue-in-cheek, bitchy yet mellow, these stories left me thinking of that well-worn phrase, "she who laughs last . . ." '
Independent on Sunday

'Laugh-out-loud funny. Weldon's flamboyant vision is transmitted in voices that extend from the uncertain via the self-righteous to the splendidly bitchy.'
List

'Amuses and bemuses. Irreverent humour at its best.'
Ireland on Sunday